ON THE GOLDEN PORCH

ALFRED A. KNOPF   NEW YORK   1989

ON THE
GOLDEN
PORCH

Tatyana Tolstaya

TRANSLATED BY ANTONINA W. BOUIS

Library of Congress Cataloging-in-Publication Data
Tolstaia, T. V. (Tat'iana Vladimirovna)
On the golden porch.
Translation of: Na zolotom kryl'tse sideli.
I. Title.
PG3476.T58N313 1989   891.73'44   88-45814
ISBN 0-394-57798-1

Contents

ON THE
GOLDEN
PORCH

LOVES ME, LOVES ME NOT

"The other kids get to go out by themselves, but we have to go with Maryvanna!"

"When you get to be seven, you'll get to go out alone. And you don't say 'disgusting' about an elderly person. You should be grateful to Maria Ivanovna for spending time with you."

"She doesn't watch us on purpose! And we're going to get run over, I know we are! And in the park she talks to all the old women and complains about us. And she says: 'spirit of contradiction.' "

"But you really do your best to spite her, don't you?"

"And I'll go on doing it! I'm going to tell all those stupid old women 'how *don't* you do' and '*bad*-bye.' "

ON THE GOLDEN PORCH   4

"Shame on you! You must have respect for your elders!
Don't be rude, listen to what they say: they're older and know
more than you."

"I do listen! All Maryvanna talks about is her uncle."

"And what does she say about him?"

"That he hanged himself because he had a bad bladder.
And that before that he was run over by the wheel of fortune.
Because he was in debt and had crossed the street im-
properly."

. . . Small, heavyset, and short of breath, Maryvanna hates
us and we hate her. We hate the hat with a veil, the holey
glove, the dried pieces of "sand cookies" she feeds to the
pigeons, and we stamp our feet at those pigeons to scare them
off. Maryvanna takes us out every day for four hours, reads
books to us, and tries to converse in French—basically, that's
what she is hired for. Because our own dear beloved Nanny
Grusha, who lives with us, doesn't know any foreign lan-
guages, and doesn't go outside anymore, and has trouble
getting around. Pushkin loved her very much, too, and wrote
about her and called her "my ancient dove." And he didn't
write anything about Maryvanna. And if he had, he'd have
written "my fat piggy."

But what's amazing—absolutely impossible to imagine—is
that Maryvanna was the beloved nanny of a now grownup girl.
And Maryvanna brings up that girl, Katya, every day. She
didn't stick out her tongue, didn't pick her nose, ate everything on her plate, and hugged and kissed Maryvanna—she
was crazy.

At night, in bed, my sister and I make up conversations
between Maryvanna and the obedient Katya.

"Finish up the worms, dear Katya."

"With pleasure, sweet Maryvanna."

"Eat a marinated frog, child."

"I already have. Please give me some more mashed mice."

In the park that Maryvanna called "the boulevard," pale Leningrad girls dig in the darkened autumn sand, listening to adults talk. Maryvanna, quickly making the acquaintance of some old lady in a hat, takes out her stiff old photographs: herself and Uncle leaning against a grand piano and behind them a waterfall. Could that white airy creature in lace gloves be buried somewhere in the bowels of that gasping fat? "He was father and mother to me and wanted me to call him simply Georges. He educated me, he brought me out into society. Those pearls—you can't see them well here—were a gift from him. He loved me madly, madly. See how handsome he is here? And here we're in Piatigorsk. That's my friend Yulya. And here we're having tea in the garden."

"Marvelous pictures. Is that Yulya too?"

"No, that's Zinaida. Georges' girlfriend. She's the one who bankrupted him. He was a gambler."

"Oh, so that's it."

"Yes. I should throw away this picture, but I can't. It's all I have left of him. And his poems—he was a poet."

"You don't say."

"Yes, yes, a wonderful poet. There aren't any like him nowadays. So romantic, a bit of a mystic . . ."

The old lady, silly twit, listens with her mouth open and smiles dreamily, looking at me. She shouldn't stare at me. I stick out my tongue. Maryvanna, shutting her eyes in shame, whispers hatefully, "Hideous creature!"

That night she'll read her uncle's poetry to me again:

> *Nanny, who screamed so loudly outside,*
> *Flashing past the window,*
> *Creaking the porch door,*
> *Sighing under the bed?*

Sleep, don't worry,
God will watch over you,
Those were ravens calling,
Flying to the cemetery.

Nanny, who touched the candle,
Who's scratching in the corner,
Who's stretched in a black shadow
On the floor from the door?

Sleep, child, don't worry,
The door is strong, the fence is high,
The thief won't escape the block
The axe will thud in the night.

Nanny, who's breathing down my back,
Who's invisible and climbing
Ever closer up my
Crumpled bed sheet?

Oh child, don't frown
Wipe your tears and don't cry.
The ropes are pulled tight,
The executioner knows his job.

Well, after hearing a poem like that, who'd be brave
enough to lower her feet from the bed, to use the potty, say?
Everybody knows that under the bed, near the wall, is the
Snake: in laceup shoes, cap, gloves, motorcycle goggles, and
holding a crook in his hand. The Snake isn't there during the
day, but he coagulates by night from twilight stuff and waits
very quietly: who will dare lower a leg? And out comes the
crook! He's unlikely to eat you, but he'll pull you in and shove
you under the plinth, and you'll fall endlessly, under the floor,
between the dusty partitions. The room is guarded by other
species of nocturnal creatures: the fragile and translucent Dry

One, weak but terrible, who stands all night in the closet and in the morning goes into the cracks. Behind the peeling wallpaper are Indrik and Hindrik: one is greenish and the other gray, and they both run fast and have many feet. And in the corner on the floor is a rectangle of copper grating, and under that a black abyss: "ventilation." It's dangerous to approach even in the daytime; the Eyes stare out, without blinking. Yes, the most horrible is the nameless one who is always behind me, almost touching my hair (Uncle knows!). Many times he plans to reach out, but he keeps missing his chance and slowly, sadly, lowers his incorporeal hands. I wrap myself tight in the blanket, only my nose sticking out—they don't attack from the front.

Having frightened me with her uncle's poems, Maryvanna goes back to her place in a communal apartment, where, besides her, live Iraida Anatolyevna with her diabetes, and dusty Sonya, and the Badylovs, who were deprived of parental rights, and the hanged uncle. . . . And she'll be back tomorrow if we don't get sick. We often are.

Many times, 104-degree flus would scream and bang at my ears, banging on red drums, surrounding me from eight sides and, swirling wildly, project a delirious film, always the same: a wooden honeycomb filling up with three-digit numbers; more numbers, louder noise, more urgent drums—all the cells will be filled now, just a little time left. My heart can't take any more, it'll burst—but it's been postponed, I've been released, forgiven, the honeycomb taken away, a round loaf of bread with a nasty smile runs along an airfield on spindly legs—and it grows quiet . . . except for tiny planes like dots of bugs which scurry along the pink sky, carrying away the black cloak of fever in their claws. It's passed.

Shake the crumbs from my sheet, cool my pillow, smooth my blanket so that there isn't a single wrinkle, otherwise the planes with claws will be back. Without thoughts, without

desires, I lie on my back, in the coolness, in semidarkness—a
half-hour's breather between two attacks of the drummers. A
fan of light crosses the ceiling from corner to corner, then
another fan, and another. The cars have their headlights on,
the evening has descended, a rug of light has been pushed
under the door into the next room: they're having tea there,
the orange lamp shade is glowing, and one of the adults is
making forbidden braids in its fringe, "ruining it." Before the
planes come back, I can leave my corporeal shell pounding
with fever among the cast-iron sheets and mentally slip beyond
the door—long nightgown, cold slippers—sit invisibly at the
table (I'd forgotten this cup over the week) and, squinting,
travel by gaze along the orange humps of the shade. The lamp
shade is young and skittish, it isn't used to me yet—Papa and
I got it only recently at the flea market.

Oh, there were so many people there, so many owners of
quilted cotton and plush jackets, of brown Orenburg scarves.
And they all gabbled and bustled and shook blue diagonal
remnants before Papa's face and shoved sturdy black felt boots
in his nose. Such treasures there! And Papa: he blew it, missed
out, he didn't bring back anything but the lamp shade. He
should have bought up everything: vases and saucers and
flowered scarves, stuffed owls and porcelain pigs and rag rugs.
We could have used the pussycat banks, and whistles and
paper flowers—poppies with inked cotton in their centers—
and paper fans, red and green trembling jabots on two sticks:
you turn the sticks out and the fringed, impermanent lace
shakes, turn them some more and it folds back up and
disappears. Marvelous oilcloth paintings flickered: Lermontov
on a gray wolf snatching up a swooning beauty; or him again
wearing a caftan and aiming from bushes at swans with gold
crowns; or doing something on a horse . . . but Papa dragged
me on, farther, farther, past invalids with lollipops, to the
lamp shade row.

A man grabbed Papa's leather sleeve, "Master, sell me your coat!"

Don't bother us with nonsense, we need a lamp shade, we have to get over there; I turn my head, I glimpse brooms, baskets, painted wooden eggs, a piglet—watch it, that's it, let's go back. Where is it? Oh, there. We push our way back through the crowd, Papa has the lamp shade, still dark and silent, but already a member of the family: it's ours now, one of us, we'll come to love it. And it waited quietly: where was it being taken? It didn't know that time would pass and it, once the favorite, would be mocked, cast down, discarded, exiled, and a new favorite would take its place: a fashionable white five-petaled "shorty." And then, insulted, mutilated, betrayed, it would go through the last mortification: it would serve as a crinoline in a children's play and then plunge forever into wastebin oblivion. *Sic transit gloria mundi.*

"Papa, buy me that, please."

"What is it?"

A merry, bundled-up peasant woman, glad to see a customer, is spinning in the cold, hopping up and down, stamping her felt boots, shaking the chopped-off golden braid as thick as a hawser.

"Buy it!"

"Papa, buy it!"

"Have you lost your mind? A stranger's hair! Don't even touch it—it's got lice."

Phooey, how horrible! I freeze: and really, there they are, enormous lice, each the size of a sparrow, with attentive eyes and shaggy legs and claws clutch the sheet, climb on the blanket, clap hands, louder and louder. . . . The delirium hums again, the fever screams, the fiery wheels spin: *flu!*

. . . A dark urban winter, a cold stream of air from the corridor: one of the adults is hauling in a huge striped sack of firewood to heat up the round brown water heater in the bathroom. Scat, you're underfoot, get out of the way! Hurrah, we're going to have baths today! A wooden railing is placed across the tub: heavy chipped basins, pitchers of hot water, the sharp scent of pitch soap, soaked wrinkled skin on the hands, the steamy mirror, stuffiness, the clean, ironed underwear, and *whizzz*, run down the cold corridor, and *plop!* into fresh sheets: heaven!

"Nanny, sing a song."

Nanny Grusha is terribly old. She was born in a village and then was brought up by a kindly countess. Her gray head holds thousands of stories about talking bears, and blue snakes that cure people with tuberculosis by climbing in through the chimney during the night, about Pushkin and Lermontov. And she knows for a fact that if you eat raw dough you'll fly away. And when she was five—like me—the tsar sent her a secret package to Lenin at Smolny Institute. There was a note in the package: "Surrender!" And Lenin replied: "Never!" And shot off a cannon.

Nanny sings:

> *The Terek flows over rocks,*
> *Splashing with a stagger . . .*
> *An evil Chechen crawls ashore,*
> *Sharpening his dagger . . .*

The curtain trembles on the window, a threateningly shining moon appears from behind a winter cloud; from the murky Karpovka Canal a black Chechen climbs onto the icy shore, shaggy, baring his teeth. . . .

"Sleep, my darling, sleep tight."

. . . Yes, things aren't going too well with Maryvanna. Should I be sent to a French group? They go out for walks, and get a snack, and play Lotto. Of course, send me. Hurrah! But that evening, the Frenchwoman returns the black sheep to mother.

"Madame, your child is completely unprepared. She stuck her tongue out at the other children, tore up pictures, and threw up her cream of wheat. Come back next year. Good-bye. *Au revoir.*"

"*Bad*-bye!" I shout, dragged away by my disappointed mother. "Eat your own crummy cream of wheat! *No* revoir!" ("Is that so? Well, just get out of here! Take your lousy kid!"—"Who needs it! Don't think you're so hot, madame.")

"Forgive us, please, she's really quite difficult."

"It's all right, I understand."

What a burden you are!

. . . Let's take colored pencils. If you lick the red, it gives a specially smooth, satiny color. Of course, not for long. Well, enough for Maryvanna's face. Put a huge wart here. Fine. Now the blue: a balloon and another balloon. And two columns. A black pancake on her head. In her hands, a purse; but I don't know how to draw one. There. Maryvanna's done. She's sitting on a peeling vernal bench, her galoshes spread and planted firmly, eyes shut, singing:

> *I was going ho-o-ome . . .*
> *My heart was fu-ull . . .*

Why don't you go home? Why don't you go to your precious Katya?

"Georges always bought halvah for me at Abrikosov's—remember?"

"Yes, yes, of course. . . ."

"Everything was dainty, delicate. . . ."

"Don't I know it. . . ."

"And now. Take these: I thought they were intellectuals! But they cut their bread in huge chunks."

"Yes, yes, yes . . . and I . . ."

"I always used the formal 'you' with my mother. I showed respect. But these ones, well, all right, I'm a stranger to them,

but their parents, at least their parents, but no . . . nothing
. . . And they grab at the table. Like this! With their hands,
their hands."

God! How long must we put up with each other?

And then they shut the little park to let it dry out. And we
simply walk the streets. And one day suddenly a tall thin
girl—a white mosquito—throws herself screeching on Maryvanna's neck, weeping, and caressing her shaking red face!

"My nanny! My dearest nanny!"

And look: that lump, weeping and gasping, also grabs the
girl, and they—strangers—right here before my eyes, are both
shouting and weeping over their stupid love.

"My dearest nanny!"

Hey, girl, what's the matter with you? Rub your eyes! It's
Maryvanna. Look, look, she has a wart. It's our Maryvanna,
our laughingstock: stupid, old, fat, silly.

But does love know that?

. . . Get out of here, girl! Don't hang around here . . . with
all that goopy stuff. . . . I push on, angry and tired. I'm much
better than that girl. But Maryvanna doesn't love me like her.
The world is unfair. The world is upside down. I don't
understand anything. I want to go home! But Maryvanna has
this radiant look, holds me tight by the hand, and puffs along
ahead.

"My feet hurt!"

"We'll make a circle and head back . . . soon, soon. . . ."

Unfamiliar parts. Twilight. The light air has risen and is
suspended over the houses; the dark air came out and is
standing in the doorways and arches, in the holes of the street.
An hour of depression for adults, of depression and fear for
children. I'm all alone in the world, Mama has lost me, we're
going to get lost any second, now. I'm in a panic and I clutch
Maryvanna's cold hand.

"That's where I live. There's my window—second from the corner."

Disembodied heads frown and open their mouths—they'll eat me—under every window. The heads are horrible, and the damp darkness of the archway is creepy, and Maryvanna is not family. High up, in the window, nose pressed against the dark glass, the hanged uncle waits, running his hands over the glass, peering. Bug off, uncle! You'll climb out of the Karpovka at night, disguised as an evil Chechen, grin under the moonlight—eyes rolled back into your head—and you'll run real fast on all fours over the cobblestone street, across the courtyard to the front door, into the heavy, dense dark, with bare hands up the icy steps, along the square staircase spiral, higher, higher, to our door. . . .

Hurry, hurry, home! To Nanny! O Nanny Grusha! Darling! Hurry to you! I've forgotten your face. I'll huddle against your dark skirts, and your warm old hands will warm my frozen, lost, bewildered heart.

Nanny will unwind my scarf, unfasten the button digging into my flesh, and take me into the cavelike warmth of the nursery, where there's a red night light, where there are soft mountains of beds, and my bitter childish tears will drip into the light blue plate of self-important kasha, so pleased with itself. And seeing that, Nanny will also cry, and sit close, and hug me, and won't ask but understand with her heart, the way an animal understands an animal, an old person a child, and a wordless creature its fellow.

Lord, the world is so frightening and hostile, the poor homeless, inexperienced soul huddling in the square in the night wind. Who was so cruel, who filled me with love and hate, fear and depression, pity and shame, but didn't give me words: stole speech, sealed my mouth, put on iron padlocks, and threw away the keys.

Maryvanna, having had her fill of tea and feeling cheerier, drops by the nursery to say good night. Why is this child crying? Come on, come on. What happened? Cut yourself? Stomachache? Punished?

(No, no, that's not it. Shut up, you don't understand! It's just that in the light blue plate, on the bottom the geese and swans are going to catch the running children, and the girl's hands are chipped off and she can't cover her head or hold her brother.)

"Come on, wipe those tears, shame on you, you're a big girl now! Clean up your plate. And I'll read you a poem."

Elbowing Maryvanna aside, lifting his top hat and squinting, Uncle Georges comes forward:

> *Not white tulips*
> *In bridal lace—*
> *It's the foam of the ocean*
> *On distant shores.*
>
> *The ship creaks*
> *Its ancient wood.*
> *Unheard of pleasures*
> *Beyond the foam.*
>
> *Not black tulips—*
> *It's women in the night.*
> *Noon passions*
> *Are hot at midnight too.*
>
> *Roll out the barrel!*
> *The native women are fine!*
> *We've waited for this night—*
> *Let's find our pleasure!*
>
> *Not crimson tulips*
> *Floating on his chest—*
> *The captain's camisole*
> *Has three holes in front;*

The merry sailors
Grin on the ocean floor . . .
The women in that country
Had beautiful hair.

"What horrors at bedtime for the child," grumbles Nanny.

The uncle bows and leaves. Maryvanna shuts the door behind herself: until tomorrow.

Go away all of you, leave me alone, you don't understand anything.

A prickly ball spins in my chest, and unspoken words bubble on my lips, smeared by tears. The red night light nods. Why, she has a fever, someone far far away cries, but he can't shout over the noise of wings, geese and swans attacking from the noisy sky.

. . . The kitchen door is shut. The sun breaks through the matte glass. Noon spills gold onto the parquet floor. Silence. Beyond the door Maryvanna weeps, and complains about us.

"I can't take any more! What is this—day after day, it gets worse . . . contrary, spiteful. . . . I've lived a hard life, always among strangers, and I've been treated in many ways, of course. . . . No, the terms—I'm not complaining, the terms are fine, but at my age . . . and with my health . . . Where does that spirit of contradiction, that hostility come from. . . . I wanted a little poetry, loftiness. . . . Useless . . . I can't take any more. . . ."

She's leaving us.

Maryvanna is leaving us. Maryvanna blows her nose into a tiny handkerchief. She powders her red nose, stares deeply into the mirror, hesitates, seems to be seeking something in its inaccessible, sealed universe. And really, deep in its twilight forgotten curtains stir, candle flames flicker, and the pale uncle comes out with a black piece of paper in his hands.

Princess Rose grew weary of life
And ended it at sunset.
She wet her lips sadly
With poisoned wine.

And the prince froze like a statue
In the grim power of sorrow,
And the retinue whispers condolences
That she was innocent.

The porphyry parents
Had their heralds announce
That the grieving populace
Lower flags in the towers.

I enter the funeral procession
As a funereal violin,
I place narcissus on the princess's
Grave with a melancholy smile.

And pretending sorrow,
I lower my eyes, so that they cannot see:
What a wedding awaits me!
You've never seen its like.

The chandeliers are covered with deathly white netting, and the mirrors with black. Maryvanna pulls down her heavy veil, gathers the ruins of her purse with trembling hands, turns and leaves, her worn shoes scuffing over the doorsill, beyond the limit, forever out of our lives.

Spring is still weak, but the snow is gone, and the remaining black crusts lie only in stone corners. It's warm in the sunshine.

Farewell, Maryvanna!

We're ready for summer.

OKKERVIL RIVER

When the sun moved into the sign of Scorpio, it grew very windy, dark, and rainy. The wet, streaming city, banging wind against the glass outside the defenseless, uncurtained, bachelor's window with processed cheeses cooling between the panes on the sill, seemed to be Peter's evil plan, the revenge of the huge, bug-eyed, big-mouthed and toothy carpenter-tsar, ship's axe in his upraised hand, chasing and gaining on his weak and terrified subjects in their nightmares. The rivers, rushing out to the windblown and threatening sea, bucked and with hissing urgency opened the cast-iron hatches and quickly raised their watery backs in museum cellars, licking at the fragile collections that were crumbling into damp sand, at shamans' masks made of rooster feathers, at crooked foreign swords, at beaded robes, and at the sinewy feet of the angry museum staff brought from their beds in the middle of the night. On days like that, when the rain, darkness, and window-bending wind reflected the white solemn face of loneliness, Simeonov, feeling particularly big-nosed and balding and particularly feeling his years around his face and his cheap socks far below, on the edge of existence, would put on the teakettle, wipe dust with his sleeve from the table, clearing away the books that stuck out their white bookmark tongues, set up the gramophone, selecting the right-sized book to support its listing side, and in blissful anticipation pull out Vera Vasilevna from the torn and yellow-stained jacket—an old and heavy disc, anthracite in color, and not disfigured by smooth concentric circles—one love song on each side.

"No! it's not you! I love! so passionately!" Vera Vasilevna skipped, creaking and hissing, quickly spinning under the needle; the hiss creak and spin formed a black tunnel that widened into the gramophone horn, and triumphant in her victory over Simeonov, speeding out of the festooned orchid of her voice, divine, low, dark, lacy and dusty at first and then throbbing with underwater pressure, rising up from the depths, transforming, trembling on the water like flames—*pshsts-pshsts-pshsts, pshsts-pshsts-pshsts*—filling like a sail, getting louder, breaking hawsers, speeding unrestrained *pshsts-pshsts-pshsts* a caravel over the nocturnal waters splashing flames—stronger—spreading its wings, gathering speed, smoothly tearing away from the remaining bulk of the flow that had given birth to it, away from the tiny Simeonov left on shore, his balding bare head lifted to the gigantic, glowing, dimming half sky to the voice coming in a triumphant cry—no, it wasn't he whom Vera Vasilevna loved so passionately, but

still, essentially, she loved only him, and it was mutual.
Kh-shch-shch-shch.

Simeonov carefully removed the now silent Vera Vasilevna,
shaking the record, holding it between straightened, respectful
hands; he examined the ancient label: Ah, where are you now,
Vera Vasilevna? Where are your white bones now? And
turning her over on her back, he placed the needle, squinting
at the olive-black shimmer of the bobbing thick disc, and
listened once more, longing for the long-faded, *pshsts,* chrysanthemums in the garden, *pshsts,* where they had met, and
once again, gathering underwater pressure, throwing off dust,
laces, and years, Vera Vasilevna creaked and appeared as a
languorous naiad—an unathletic, slightly plump turn-of-
the-century naiad—O sweet pear, guitar, hourglass, slope-
hipped champagne bottle!

And by then the teakettle would be aboil, and Simeonov,
fishing some processed cheese or ham scraps from the windowsill, would put the record on again and have a bachelor feast off
a newspaper, delighting in the fact that Tamara would not find
him today, would not disturb his precious rendezvous with
Vera Vasilevna. He was happy alone in his small apartment,
alone with Vera Vasilevna. The door was securely locked
against Tamara, and the tea was strong and sweet, and the
translation of the unneeded book from the rare language was
almost complete—he would have money soon, and Simeonov
would buy a scarce record from a shark for a high price, one
where Vera Vasilevna regrets that spring will come but not
for her—a man's romance, a romance of solitude, and the
incorporeal Vera Vasilevna will sing it, merging with Simeonov into a single longing, sobbing voice. O blessed solitude!
Solitude eats right out of the frying pan, spears a cold meat
patty from a murky half-liter jar, makes tea right in the
mug—so what? Peace and freedom! A family rattles the dish

cupboard, sets out traps of cups and saucers, catches your soul with knife and fork—gets it under the ribs from both sides—smothers it with a tea caddy, tosses a tablecloth over its head, but the free lone soul slips out through the linen fringe, squeezes like an eel through the napkin ring and—*hop! catch me if you can!*—it's back in the dark magical circle filled with flames, outlined by Vera Vasilevna's voice, following her skirts and fan from the bright ballroom out onto the summer balcony at night, the spacious semicircle above a sweet-smelling bed of chrysanthemums; well, actually, their white, dry, and bitter aroma is an autumnal one, a harbinger of fall separation, oblivion, but love still lives in my ailing heart—a sickly smell, the smell of sadness and decay, *where are you now, Vera Vasilevna,* perhaps in Paris or Shanghai and which rain— Parisian light blue or Chinese yellow—drizzles over your grave, and whose soil chills your white bones? *No, it's not you I love so passionately.* (That's what you say. Of course it's me, Vera Vasilevna.)

Trolleys passed Simeonov's window, once upon a time clanging their bells and swinging the hanging loops that resembled stirrups—Simeonov kept thinking that the horses were hidden up in the ceiling, like portraits of trolley ancestors taken up to the attic; but the bells grew still, and now all he heard was the rattle, clickety-clack and squeals on the turns, and at last the red-sided cars with wooden benches died, and the new cars were rounded, noiseless, hissing at stops, and you could sit, plopping down on the soft seat that gasped and gave up the ghost beneath you, and ride off into the blue yonder to the last stop, beckoning with its name: *Okkervil River.* But Simeonov had never gone there. It was the end of the world and there was nothing there for him, but that wasn't it, really: without seeing or knowing that distant, almost non-Leningrad river, he could imagine it in any way he chose: a murky

greenish flow, for instance, with a slow green sun murkily
floating in it, silvery willows softly hanging down from the
gentle bank, red brick two-story houses with tile roofs,
humped wooden bridges—a quiet world in a sleepy stupor;
but actually it was probably filled with warehouses, fences,
and some stinking factory spitting out mother-of-pearl toxic
gases, a dump smoldering smelly smoke, or something else
hopeless, provincial, and trite. No, no reason to be disillu-
sioned by going to Okkervil River, it was better to mentally
plant long-haired willows on its banks, set up steep-roofed
houses, release slow-moving residents, perhaps in German
caps, striped stockings, with long porcelain pipes in their
mouths. . . . even better to pave the Okkervil's embankment,
fill the river with gray water, sketch in bridges with towers
and chains, smooth out the granite parapets with a curved
template, line the embankment with tall gray houses with cast
iron grates on the windows—with a fish-scale motif on top of
the gates and nasturtiums peeking from the balconies—and
settle young Vera Vasilevna there and let her walk, pulling on
a long glove, along the paving stones, placing her feet close
together, stepping daintily with her black snub-toed slippers
with apple-round heels, in a small round hat with a veil,
through the still drizzle of a St. Petersburg morning; and in
that case, make the fog light blue.

Let's have light blue fog. The fog in place, Vera Vasilevna
walks, her round heels clicking, across the entire paved section
held in Simeonov's imagination, here's the edge of the scenery,
the director's run out of means, he is powerless and weary, he
releases the actors, crosses out the balconies with nasturtiums,
gives those who like it the grating with fish-scale motif, flicks
the granite parapets into the water, stuffs the towered bridges
into his pockets—the pockets bulge, the chains droop as if
from grandfather's watch, and only the Okkervil River flows

on, narrowing and widening feverishly, unable to select a permanent image for itself.

Simeonov ate processed cheese, translated boring books, sometimes brought women home in the evenings and in the morning, disappointed, saw them out—*no! it's not you!*—hid from Tamara, who kept coming over with washed laundry and fried potatoes and flowered curtains for the windows, and who assiduously kept forgetting important things at Simeonov's— hairpins or a handkerchief she needed urgently by nightfall, and she would travel across the whole city to get them, and Simeonov would put out the light and stand pressed against the foyer wall while she banged on the door, and very often he gave in, and then he had a hot meal for dinner and drank strong tea from a blue and gold cup and had homemade cookies for dessert, and it was too late for Tamara to go back home, of course; the last trolley had gone and it wouldn't reach the foggy Okkervil River, and Tamara would fluff up the pillows while Vera Vasilevna—turning her back and not listening to Simeonov's explanations—would walk into the night along the embankment, swaying on her apple-round heels.

The autumn was thickening when he purchased a heavy disc, chipped on one side, from a shark—they had haggled over the damage, the price was very high, and why? because Vera Vasilevna was forgotten, was never played on the radio, never flashed in a newsreel, and now only refined eccentrics, snobs, amateurs, and aesthetes who felt like throwing money on the incorporeal chased after her records, collected wire recordings, transcribed her low, dark voice that glowed like aged wine. *The old woman's still alive,* the shark said, she lives somewhere in Leningrad, in poverty, they say, and shabbiness, she didn't shine too long in her day, either; she lost her diamonds, husband, apartment, son, two lovers, and finally her voice: in that order; and she managed to handle all those losses before she was thirty-five, and she stopped singing back then, though she's still alive. So that's how it is, thought Simeonov with heavy heart on the way home over bridges and through gardens, across trolley tracks, thinking *that's how it is*. . . . And locking the door, making tea, he put on his newly acquired treasure and, looking out the window at the heavy colored clouds looming on the sunset side, built, as usual, a section of the granite embankment, erected a bridge: the towers were heavier this time, and the chains were very cast iron, and the wind ruffled and wrinkled, agitated the broad gray smoothness of the Okkervil River, and Vera Vasilevna, tripping more than she ought in her uncomfortable heels invented by Simeonov, wrung her hands and bent her neatly coiffed head toward her sloping little shoulder—the moon glowed so softly, so softly, and my thoughts are full of you—the moon wouldn't cooperate and slipped out like soap from his hands, sliding across the Okkervil clouds—there were always problems with the Okkervil skies—how restlessly the transparent, tamed shadows of our imagination scurry when the noises and smells of real life penetrate into their cool, foggy world.

Looking at the sunset rivers where the Okkervil River also had its source, already blooming with toxic greenery, already poisoned by the living breath of an old woman, Simeonov listened to the arguing voices of two struggling demons: one demanded he throw the old woman out of his head, lock the door—opening it occasionally for Tamara—and go on as before, loving moderately, longing moderately, in moments of solitude listening to the pure sound of the silver horn singing over the unknown foggy river; the other demon, a wild youth with a mind dimmed by translating bad books, demanded that he walk, *run,* to find Vera Vasilevna, a half-blind, impoverished, emaciated, hoarse, stick-legged old woman; find her, bend over her almost deaf ear and shout through the years and misfortunes that she is the one and only, that he had passionately loved her always, that love still lives in his ailing heart, that she, the divine Peri, her voice rising from underwater depths, filling sails, speeding along the flaming waters of the night, surging upward, eclipsing half the sky, had destroyed and uplifted him—Simeonov, her faithful knight—and crushed by her silvery voice, the trolleys, books, processed cheeses, wet sidewalks, bird calls, Tamaras, cups, nameless women, passing years, and the weight of the world all rolled off like tiny pieces of gravel. And the old woman, stunned, would look at him with tear-filled eyes: What? You know me? It can't be! My God! does anyone still care? I never thought—and bewildered, she wouldn't know where to seat Simeonov, while tenderly holding her elbow and kissing her no longer white hand, covered with age spots, he would lead her to an armchair, peering into her faded face of old-fashioned bone structure. And looking at the part in her thin white hair with tenderness and pity, he would think: Oh, how we missed each other in this world. What madness that time separated us. ("Ugh, *don't*," grimaced his inner demon, but Simeonov wanted to do what was right.)

He obtained Vera Vasilevna's address in the most mundane and insulting way—for five kopeks at a sidewalk directory kiosk. His heart thumped: would it be Okkervil? of course not. And not the embankment either. He bought chrysanthemums at the market—tiny yellow ones wrapped in cellophane. Long faded. And he picked up a cake at the bakery. The saleswoman took off the cardboard cover and showed him his selection on her outstretched hand: will it do?—but Simeonov did not notice what he was buying and recoiled, because Tamara was outside the bakery window—or was it his imagination?—going to get him, nice and warm, in his apartment. Only in the trolley did he untie his purchase and look inside. Not bad. Fruit. Decent looking. Lone fruits slept in the corners under a glassy gel: a slice of apple here; in a more expensive corner a chunk of peach; here half a plum frozen in eternal cold; here a mischievous, ladylike corner with three cherries. The sides were dusted with confectionery dandruff. The trolley jolted, the cake slipped, and Simeonov saw a clear thumbprint on the smooth jellied surface—either the careless baker's or the clumsy saleswoman's. No problem, the old woman doesn't see well. I'll cut it up right away. ("Go back"—his guardian demon sadly shook his head—"run for your life.") Simeonov retied the box as best he could and began looking at the sunset. The Okkervil rushed noisily in a narrow stream, slapping the granite shores, and the shores crumbled like sand and crept into the water. He stood before Vera Vasilevna's house, shifting the presents from hand to hand. The gates he had to pass were ornamented with a fish-scale motif. Beyond: a horrible courtyard. A cat scurried by. Just as I thought. A great forgotten artist has to live off a courtyard like this. The back entrance, garbage cans, narrow iron banisters, dirt. His heart was pounding. Long faded. *In my ailing heart.*

He rang. (*"Fool,"* said his inner demon, spat, and left Simeonov.) The door was flung open by the onslaught of noise, singing, and laughter pouring out of the apartment, and Vera Vasilevna appeared, white and huge, rouged, with thick black brows; appeared at the set table in the illuminated segment above a mound of sharply spiced hors d'oeuvres he could smell even from the doorway, above an enormous chocolate cake crowned with a chocolate bunny, laughing loudly, raucously; appeared and was selected by fate forever. He should have turned and left. Fifteen people at the table laughed, watching her: it was Vera Vasilevna's birthday, and Vera Vasilevna, gasping with laughter, was telling a joke. She had begun telling it while Simeonov was going up the stairs, she was already cheating on him with those fifteen people while he fumbled and worried at the gate, shifting the defective cake from hand to hand, while he was still in the trolley, while he was locking himself in his apartment and clearing space on his dirty table for her silvery voice, while he was taking the heavy black disc with its moonlight radiance from the yellow jacket the very first time; even before he was born, when there was only wind rustling grass and silence reigned in the world. She was not waiting for him, thin, at the lancet window, peering into the distance into the glassy streams of the Okkervil River; she was laughing in a low voice over a table crowded with dishes, over salads, cucumbers, fish, and bottles, and she drank dashingly, the enchantress, and she turned her heavy body dashingly, too. She had betrayed him. Or had he betrayed Vera Vasilevna? It was too late to figure out now.

"Another one!" someone shouted laughingly, a man, he learned immediately, with the surname Kissov. "You have to pay a fine." They took the fingerprinted cake and the flowers from Simeonov and squeezed him in at the table, making him drink to the health of Vera Vasilevna, health, as he was convinced, being the last thing she needed. Simeonov sat, smiling automatically, nodding, stabbing a pickled tomato with his fork, watching Vera Vasilevna like everyone else, listening to her loud jokes—his life was crushed, run over into two; it was his own fault, it was too late now; the magical diva had been abducted, she had allowed herself to be abducted, she hadn't given a damn about the handsome sad balding prince promised her by fate, she didn't wish to listen for his steps in the noise of the rain and the howling wind outside the autumn windowpanes, didn't wish to sleep enchanted for a hundred years after pricking her finger, she had surrounded herself with mortal, edible people, had made a friend of that horrible Kissov—made even closer, horribly, intimately, by the sound of his name—and Simeonov trampled the tall gray houses by Okkervil River, crushed the bridges with their towers and tossed away the chains, poured garbage into the clear gray water; but the river found itself a new course, and the houses stubbornly rose from the ruins, and carriages pulled by a pair of bays traveled over the bridges.

"Have a smoke?" Kissov asked. "I quit, so I don't carry any." He relieved Simeonov of half a pack. "Who are you? An adoring fan? That's good. Have your own place? With your own bath? *Gut*. She has to share one here. You'll bring her to your place to bathe. She likes to take baths. We gather on the first of the month and listen to recordings. What do you have? Have you got 'Dark Green Emerald'? Too bad. We've been looking for it for years. It's awful—nowhere to be had. The ones you have were hits, lots of them around, that's not interesting. Look for 'Emerald.' Have you any connections for getting smoked sausage? No, it's bad for her, it's for . . . me. You couldn't find any punier flowers? I brought roses, they were the size of my fist." Kissov brought his hairy fist close. "You're not a journalist, are you? It would be great to have a radio show on her, our little Vera keeps hoping for that. What a face. But her voice is still as strong as a deacon's. Let me write down your address."

He squashed Simeonov into the chair with his big hand, "Don't get up, I'll see myself out," Kissov got up from the table and left, taking Simeonov's cake with the dactyloscopic memento.

Strangers instantly inhabited the foggy banks of the Okkervil, hauling their cheap-smelling belongings—pots and mattresses, buckets and marmalade cats; there was no space on the granite embankment, they were singing their own songs, sweeping garbage onto the paving stones laid by Simeonov, giving birth, multiplying, visiting one another; the fat black-browed old woman knocked down the pale shadow with its sloping shoulders, crushed the veiled hat under her foot, and the old-fashioned round heels fell in different directions, and Vera Vasilevna shouted across the table, "Pass the mushrooms!" and Simeonov passed them and she ate some.

He watched her big nose move, and the mustache under it, watched her large black eyes veiled with a film of age travel from face to face when someone turned on a tape recorder and her silvery voice floated out, gathering strength—it's all right, thought Simeonov. I'll get home soon, it's all right. Vera Vasilevna died, she died long, long ago, killed, dismembered and eaten by this old woman, the bones were sucked clean, I could enjoy the wake but Kissov took away my cake; but it's all right, here are chrysanthemums for the grave, dry sick dead flowers, very appropriate, I've commemorated the dead, now I can get up and leave.

Tamara—the darling!—was hanging around by Simeonov's door. She picked him up, carried him in, washed him, undressed him and fed him a hot meal. He promised Tamara he would marry her but toward morning, in his sleep, Vera Vasilevna came, spat in his face, called him names, and went down the damp embankment into the night, swaying on the black heels he had invented. In the morning Kissov knocked and rang at the door, come to examine the bathroom, to prepare it for the evening. And in the evening he brought Vera Vasilevna to bathe at Simeonov's, smoked Simeonov's cigarettes, devoured sandwiches, and said, "Ye-e-es . . . our little Vera is a force! Think how many men she devoured in her time—my God!" And against his will Simeonov listened to the creaks and splashes of Vera Vasilevna's heavy body in the

cramped tub, how her soft, heavy, full hip pulled away from
the side of the damp tub with a *slurp,* how the water drained
with a sucking gurgle, how her bare feet padded on the floor
and at last, throwing back the hook, out came a red parboiled
Vera Vasilevna in a robe, *"Oof.* That was good." Kissov
hurried with the tea, and Simeonov, enchanted, smiling, went
to rinse off after Vera Vasilevna, to use the flexible shower
hose to wash the gray pellets of skin from the tub's drying
walls, to scoop the white hairs from the drain. Kissov wound
up the gramophone, and the divine stormy voice, gaining
strength, rose in a crescendo from the depths, spread its wings,
soared above the world, above the steamy body of little Vera
drinking tea from the saucer, above Simeonov bent in his
lifelong obedience, above warm, domestic Tamara, above
everyone beyond help, above the approaching sunset, the
gathering rain, the wind, the nameless rivers flowing back-
wards, overflowing their banks, raging and flooding the city
as only rivers can.

SWEET
SHURA

The first time Alexandra Ernestovna passed me it was early spring, and she was gilded by the pink Moscow sun. Stockings sagging, shoes shabby, black suit shiny and frayed. But her hat! . . . The four seasons—snow balls, lilies of the valley, cherries, and barberries—were entwined on the pale straw platter fastened to the remainder of her hair with a pin *this* big. The cherries dropped down and clicked against each other. She has to be ninety, I thought. But I was off by six years. The sunny air ran down a sunbeam from the roof of the cool old building and then ran back up, up, where we rarely look— where the iron balcony hangs suspended in the uninhabited heights, where there is a steep roof, a delicate fretwork erected right in the morning sky, a melting tower, a spire, doves, angels—no, I don't see so well. Smiling blissfully, eyes clouded by happiness, Alexandra Ernestovna moves along the sunny side, moving her prerevolutionary legs in wide arcs. Cream, a roll, carrots in a net bag weigh down her arm and rub against the heavy black hem of her suit. The wind had walked from the south smelling of sea and roses, promising a path up easy stairs to heavenly blue countries. Alexandra Ernestovna smiles at the morning, at me. The black clothing, the light hat with clicking dead fruit, vanish around the corner.

Later I came across her sitting on the broiling boulevard—limp, but admiring a sweaty, solitary child marooned in the baking city; she never had children of her own. A horrible slip showed beneath her tattered black skirt. The strange child trustingly dumped his sandy treasures onto Alexandra Ernestovna's lap. Don't dirty the lady's clothing. It's all right. . . . Let him.

I saw her in the stifling air of the movie theater (take off your hat, granny! we can't see!). Out of rhythm with the screen passions, Alexandra Ernestovna breathed noisily, rattled foil candy wrappers, gluing together her frail, store-bought teeth with sweet goo.

Later she was swirled in the flow of fire-breathing cars by the Nikitsky Gates, got flustered and lost her sense of direction, clutched my arm and floated out onto the saving shore, losing forever the respect of the black diplomat behind the green windshield of a low, shiny car and of his pretty, curly-haired children. The black man roared and raced off in the direction of the conservatory with a puff of blue smoke, while Alexandra Ernestovna, trembling, bent over, eyes popping, hung on to me and dragged me off to her communal refuge—bric-a-brac, oval frames, dried flowers—leaving behind a trail of smelling salts.

Two tiny rooms, a high ornate ceiling, and on the peeling walls a charming beauty smiles, muses, pouts—sweet Shura, Alexandra Ernestovna. *Yes, yes, that's me!* In a hat, without a hat, with hair down. Oh, so beautiful. . . . And that's her second husband, and well, that's her third—not a very good choice. But what can you do about it now. . . . Now, if she had made the decision to run off with Ivan Nikolayevich then . . . Who is Ivan Nikolayevich? He's not here, he's crammed into the album, spread-eagled in four slits in the cardboard, squashed by a lady in a bustle, crushed by some short-lived white lap dogs that died before the Russo-Japanese War.

Sit down, sit down, what would you like? . . . Please come visit, of course, please do. Alexandra Ernestovna is all alone in the world, and it would be so nice to chat.

. . . Autumn. Rain. Alexandra Ernestovna, do you remember me? It's me! Remember . . . well, it doesn't matter, I've come to visit. Visit—ah, how wonderful! Come here, this way, I'll clear . . . I still live alone. I've survived them all. Three husbands, you know? And Ivan Nikolayevich, he wanted me, but . . . Maybe I should have gone? What a long life? That's me. There too. And that's my second husband. I had three husbands, did you know? Of course, the third wasn't so . . .

The first was a lawyer. Famous. We lived very well. Finland in the spring. The Crimea in the summer. White cakes, black coffee. Hats trimmed with lace. Oysters—very expensive . . . Theater in the evening. So many admirers! He died in 1919—stabbed in an alley.

Oh, naturally she had one romance after another all her life, what else do you expect? That's a woman's heart for you. Why, just three years ago, Alexandra Ernestovna had rented the small room to a violinist. Twenty-six years old, won competitions, those eyes! . . . Of course, he hid his feelings; but the eyes, they give it away. In the evenings Alexandra Ernestovna would sometimes ask him, "Some tea?" And he would just look at her and say no-o-thing in response. Well, you get it, don't you? . . . Treacherous! He kept silent all the time he lived at Alexandra Ernestovna's. But you could see he was burning up and his soul was throbbing. Alone in the evenings in those two small rooms. . . . You know, there was something in the air—we both felt it . . . He couldn't bear it and would go out. Outside. Wander around till late. Alexandra Ernestovna was steadfast and gave him no encouragement. Later—on the rebound—he married some woman, nothing special. Moved. And once after his marriage he ran into Alexandra Ernestovna on the street and cast such a look at her—he burned her to ashes. But said nothing. Kept it all bottled up in his soul.

Yes, Alexandra Ernestovna's heart had never been empty. Three husbands, by the way. She lived with her second husband in an enormous apartment before the war. A famous physician. Famous guests. Flowers. Always gay. And he died merrily: when it was clear that this was the end, Alexandra Ernestovna called in gypsies. You know, when you see beauty, noise, merriment—it's easier to die, isn't it? She couldn't find real gypsies. But Alexandra Ernestovna, inventive, did not lose heart, she hired some dark-skinned boys and girls, dressed them in rustling, shiny, swirling clothes, flung open the doors to her dying husband's bedroom—and they jangled, howled, babbled, circled and whirled and kicked: pink, gold, gold, pink. My husband didn't expect them, he had already turned his gaze inward and suddenly here they were, squealing, flashing shawls; he sat up, waved his arms, rasped: go away! But they grew louder, merrier, stamped their feet. And so he died, may he rest in peace. But the third husband wasn't so . . .

But Ivan Nikolayevich . . . ah, Ivan Nikolayevich. It was so brief: the Crimea, 1913, the striped sun shining through the blinds sawing the white scraped floor into sections . . . Sixty years passed, but still . . . Ivan Nikolayevich lost his mind: leave your husband *right now* and come to the Crimea. Forever. She promised. Then, back in Moscow, she thought: what will we live on? and where? He showered her with letters: "Sweet Shura, come, come to me!" Her husband was busy, rarely home; while there in the Crimea, on the gentle sands under the blue skies, Ivan Nikolayevich paced like a tiger: "Sweet Shura, forever!" While the poor man didn't have enough money for a ticket to Moscow. Letters, letters, every day letters for a whole year—Alexandra Ernestovna will show them to me.

Ah, how he loved me! Should I go or not?

A human life has four seasons. Spring! Summer. Autumn . . . Winter? But winter was behind Alexandra Ernestovna— where was she now? Where were her moist, colorless eyes directed? Head back, red lid pulled away, Alexandra Ernestovna squeezes yellow drops into her eyes. Her scalp shows like a pink balloon through the thin net. Could this mouse tail have been a thick black peacock tail caressing her shoulders sixty years ago? Had the persistent but poor Ivan Nikolayevich drowned in those eyes—once and for all? Alexandra Ernestovna groans and feels around with her gnarled feet for her slippers.

"We'll have some tea now. I won't let you go without a cup. No-no-no, don't even think about it."

I'm not going anywhere. That's why I dropped by—for a cup of tea. And I brought pastry. I'll put the kettle on, don't worry. And she gets the velvet-covered album and the old letters.

It was a long way to the kitchen, to another city, along an

endlessly shining floor, so polished the red paste left traces on my shoes for two days. At the end of the corridor tunnel, like a light in a deep robber forest, glowed the circle of the kitchen window. Twenty-three neighbors were silent behind the clean white doors. Halfway down was a wall telephone. A white note tacked up once upon a time by Alexandra Ernestovna: "Fire—01. Emergency—03. In case of my death call Elizaveta Osipovna." Elizaveta Osipovna herself is long gone. No matter. Alexandra Ernestovna forgot.

The kitchen is painfully, lifelessly clean. Somebody's cabbage soup talks to itself on one of the stoves. In the corner stands a curly cone of smell left by a Belomor-smoking neighbor. A chicken hangs in a net bag outside the window as if being punished, twisting in the black wind. A bare wet tree droops in grief. A drunkard unbuttons his coat, resting his face on the fence. And what if Alexandra Ernestovna had agreed to abandon everything and fly south to be with Ivan Nikolayevich? Where would she be now? She had sent a telegram (*I'm coming, meet me*), packed her things, tucked the ticket away in the secret compartment of her wallet, pinned her peacock hair up high and sat in an armchair by the window to wait. And far south, Ivan Nikolayevich, agitated, unable to believe his good fortune, rushed to the railroad station—to run, worry, fluster, give orders, hire, negotiate, lose his mind, stare at the horizon enveloped in dull heat. And then? She stayed in the armchair until evening, until the first pure stars. And then? She pulled the pins from her hair, shook her head. . . . And then? Why keep asking *and then*, and then? Life passed, that's what happened *then*.

The teakettle came to a boil. I'll make it strong. A simple piece for the kitchen xylophone: lid, lid, spoon, lid, rag, lid, rag, rag, spoon, handle, handle. It's a long way back down the long corridor with two teakettles in your hands. Twenty-three

neighbors behind white doors listen closely: will she spill her
crummy tea on our clean floor? I didn't spill, don't worry. I
push open the gothic doors with my foot. I've been gone an
eternity, but Alexandra Ernestovna still remembers me.

She got out cracked raspberry-colored cups, decorated the
table with doilies, puttered around in the dark coffin of a
cupboard, stirring up bread and cracker smells that come out
of its wooden cheeks. Don't come out, smell! Catch it and
squeeze it back with the cut-glass doors: there, stay under lock
and key.

Alexandra Ernestovna gets out *wonderful* jam, it was a gift,
just try it, no, no, *you* try it, ah, ah, ah, yes, you're speechless,
it's truly amazing, *exquisite, isn't it?* Really, in all my long life,
I've never . . . well, I'm so pleased, I knew you'd like it, have
some more, please, take it, have some, I beg you. (Damn it,
I'll have another toothache!)

I like you, Alexandra Ernestovna, I like you very much,
especially in that photograph there with that marvelous oval to
your face, and in that one, where your head is back and you
laugh with those perfect teeth, and in that one, where you
pretend to be pouting, and your arm is behind your head so
the lacy festoons will fall back from your elbow. I like your
life, interesting to no one else, passed in the distance, your
youth that rushed off, your decayed admirers and husbands
proceeding in triumphant parade, everyone who ever called
your name or was called by you, everyone who passed and went
over the high hill. I'll come to you and bring you cream, and
carrots, so good for your eyes, and you'll please open up the
long-closed brown velvet albums—let the Gymnasium girls
breathe some fresh air, let the mustachioed gentlemen flex
their muscles, let brave Ivan Nikolayevich smile. Don't
worry, don't worry, Alexandra Ernestovna, he can't see you,
really. . . . You should have done it then. You should have.
She's made up her mind. Here he is—right next to you—just

reach out! Here, take him in your hands, hold him, here he is, flat cold shiny with a gold border, slightly yellowed: Ivan Nikolayevich. Hey, do you hear, she's decided, *yes*, she's coming, meet her, she's stopped hesitating, she's made up her mind, hey, where are you, yoo-hoo!

Thousands of years, thousands of days, thousands of translucent impenetrable curtains fell from the heavens, thickened, turned into solid walls, blocked roads, and kept Alexandra Ernestovna from going to her beloved, lost in time. He remained there on the other side of the years, alone at the dusty southern station, wandering along the sunflower seed–spattered platform; he looks at his watch, kicks aside dusty corn cobs with his toe, impatiently tears off blue-gray cypress cones, waiting, waiting, waiting for the steam engine to come from the hot morning distance. She did not come. She will not come. She had deceived him. But no, no, she had wanted to go. She was ready, and the bags had been packed. The white semitransparent dresses had tucked up their knees in the cramped darkness of the trunk, the vanity case's leather sides creaked and its silver corners shone, the shameless bathing costumes barely covering the knees—baring the arms to the shoulder—awaited their hour, squinting, anticipating . . . In the hat box—impossible, enticing, insubstantial . . . ah, there are no words to describe it—white zephyr, a miracle! On the very bottom, belly-up and paws in the air, slept the sewing box—pins, combs, silk laces, emery boards of diamond sand for delicate nails; trifles. A jasmine genie sealed in a crystal flask—ah, how it would shine with a billion rainbows in the blinding seaside sun! She was ready—but what interfered? What always interferes? Well hurry, time's passing. . . . Time's passing, and the invisible layers of years get thicker, and the rails get rusty, and the roads get overgrown, and weeds grow taller in the ravines. Time flows and makes sweet Shura's boat bob on its back and splashes wrinkles into her incomparable face.

. . . More tea?

After the war she returned—with her third husband—here, to these rooms. The third husband kept whining, whining. . . . The corridor was too long. The light too dim. The windows faced the back. Everything was behind them. The festive guests died out. The flowers faded. Rain hammered at the windows. He whined and whined and died, but when and of what, Alexandra Ernestovna did not notice.

She got Ivan Nikolayevich out of the album, and looked at him a long time. How he had begged her! She had even bought a ticket—and here it was, the ticket. Hard cardboard—black numbers. If you want, look at it this way, if you want, turn it upside down. It doesn't matter: forgotten signs of an unknown alphabet, a coded pass to that shore.

Maybe if you learn the magic word . . . if you guess it; if you sit down and think hard, or look for it . . . there has to be a door, a crack, an unnoticed crooked way back there to that day; they shut up everything but they must have missed a crack somewhere: maybe in some old house, maybe if you pull back the floorboards in the attic—or in a dead end, or in a brick wall, there's a passage carelessly filled with bricks, hurriedly painted, haphazardly nailed shut with crisscrossed boards. . . . Maybe not here but in another city . . . Maybe somewhere in the tangle of rails on a siding there stands a railroad car, old and rusted, its ceiling collapsed: the one sweet Shura didn't get into?

"There's my compartment . . . Excuse me, I'll get by. Wait, here's my ticket—it says so right here." There, down in that end—rusted shock absorbers, reddish buckled wall girders, blue sky in the ceiling, grass underfoot—that's her place, right here! No one ever took it, no one had a right.

. . . More tea? A blizzard.

. . . More tea? Apple trees in bloom. Dandelions. Lilacs. Oof, it's hot. Leave Moscow—to the seaside. Until our next meeting, Alexandra Ernestovna. I'll tell you all about that part of the world. Whether the sea has dried up, whether the Crimea floated away like a dry leaf, whether the blue sky has faded. Whether your tormented, excited beloved has deserted his volunteer post at the railroad station.

In Moscow's stony hell Alexandra Ernestovna waits for me. No, no, it's all true! There, in the Crimea, the invisible but agitated Ivan Nikolayevich—in white uniform—paces up and down the dusty platform, digs his watch out of his pocket, wipes his shaved neck; up and down along the lattice work fence rubbing off white dust, oblivious and agitated; past him, without noticing, go beautiful, large-faced young women in trousers; hippie boys with their sleeves rolled up, enveloped in transistorized badoobadooms; farm women in white scarves with buckets of plums; southern ladies with plastic earrings; old men in unyielding synthetic hats; smashing right through Ivan Nikolayevich, but he doesn't know, doesn't notice, doesn't care, he's waiting, time has been derailed, stuck midway somewhere outside of Kursk, tripped on nightingale rivers, lost, blind in fields of sunflowers.

Ivan Nikolayevich, wait! I'll tell her, I'll give her the message; don't leave, she'll come, she'll come, *honest;* she's made up her mind, she's willing, just stand there, *don't worry,* she'll be here soon, she's packed, she just has to pick it up; she's even got a ticket: I swear, I've seen it—in the velvet album tucked behind a photograph; it's a bit worn of course, but don't worry, I think they'll let her on. There's a problem back there, something's in the way, I don't remember what; but she'll manage, she'll think of something—she's got the ticket, doesn't she?—that's important, the ticket, and you know the main thing is she's made up her mind, it's certain, I'm telling you.

Alexandra Ernestovna's signal is five rings, third button from the top. There's a breeze on the landing: the dusty

stairwell windows are open, ornamented with easygoing
lotuses—the flowers of oblivion.

"Who? . . . She died."

What do you mean . . . just a minute . . . why? . . . I just
. . . I just went there and came back. Are you serious? . . .
The hot white air attacks you as you come out of the
passageway crypt, trying to get you in the eyes. Wait . . . The
garbage probably hasn't been picked up, right? The spirals of
earthly existence end around the corner on a patch of asphalt,
in rubbish bins. Where did you think? Beyond the clouds,
maybe? There they are, the spirals—springs sticking out from
the rotting couch. They dumped everything here. The oval
portrait of sweet Shura—the glass broken, the eyes scratched
out. Old woman's rubbish—stockings . . . The hat with the
four seasons. Do you need chipped cherries? No? Why not? A
pitcher with a broken-off spout. The velvet album was stolen.
Naturally. It'll be good for polishing shoes. You're all so
stupid, I'm not crying. Why should I? The garbage steamed in
the hot sun and melted in a black banana ooze. The packet of
letters trampled into slush. "Sweet Shura, when will you?"
"Sweet Shura, just say the word." And one letter, drier,
swirls, a yellow lined butterfly under the dusty poplar, not
knowing where to settle.

What can I do with all this? Turn around and leave. It's
hot. The wind chases the dust around. And Alexandra
Ernestovna, sweet Shura, as real as a mirage, crowned with
wooden fruit and cardboard flowers, floats smiling along the
vibrating crossing, around the corner, southward to the
unimaginably distant shimmering south, to the lost platform,
floats, melts, and dissolves in the hot midday sun.

FOR MY SISTER, SHURA

On the golden porch sat:
Tsar, tsarevich, king, prince,
Cobbler, tailor.
Who are you?
Tell me fast, don't hold us up.

—Children's counting rhyme

ON THE GOLDEN PORCH

In the beginning was the garden. Childhood was a garden. Without end or limit, without borders and fences, in noises and rustling, golden in the sun, pale green in the shade, a thousand layers thick—from heather to the crowns of the pines: to the south, the well with toads, to the north, white roses and mushrooms, to the west, the mosquitoed raspberry patch, to the east, the huckleberry patch, wasps, the cliff, the lake, the bridges. They say that early in the morning they saw a *completely* naked man at the lake. Honest. Don't tell Mother. Do you know who it was?—It can't be.—Honest, it was. He thought he was alone. We were in the bushes.—What did you see?—*Everything.*

Now, that was luck. That happens once every hundred years. Because the only available naked man—in the anatomy textbook—isn't real. Having torn off his skin for the occasion, brazen, meaty, and red, he shows off his clavicular-sternum-nipple muscles (all dirty words!) to the students of the eighth grade. When we're promoted (in a hundred years) to the eighth grade, he'll show us all that too.

The old woman, Anna Ilyinichna, feeds her tabby cat, Memeka, with red meat like that. Memeka was born after the war and she has no respect for food. Digging her four paws into the pine tree trunk, high above the ground, Memeka is frozen in immobile despair.

"Memeka, meat, meat!"

The old woman shakes the dish of steaks, lifts it higher for the cat to see better.

"Just look at that meat!"

The cat and the old woman regard each other drearily. "Take it away," thinks Memeka.

"*Meat,* Memeka."

In the suffocating undergrowths of Persian red lilac, the cat mauls sparrows. We found a sparrow like that. Someone had scalped its toy head. A naked fragile skull like a gooseberry. A martyred sparrow face. We made it a cap of lace scraps, made it a white shroud, and buried it in a chocolate box. Life is eternal. Only birds die.

Four carefree dachas stood without fences—go wherever you want. The fifth was a privately owned house. The black log framework spread sideways from beneath the damp overhang of maples and larches and growing brighter, multiplying its windows, thinning out into sun porches, pushing aside nasturtiums, jostling lilacs, avoiding hundred-year-old firs, it ran out laughing onto the southern side and sopped above the smooth strawberry-dahlia slope *down-down-down* where warm

air trembles and the sun breaks up on the open glass lids of
magical boxes filled with cucumber babies inside rosettes of
orange flowers.

By the house (and what was inside?), having flung open all
the windows of the July-pierced veranda, Veronika Vikentievna, a huge white beauty, weighs strawberries: for jam and
for sale to neighbors. Luxurious, golden, applelike beauty!
White hens cluck at her heavy feet, turkey-cocks stick their
indecent faces out of the burdock, a red-and-green rooster
cocks his head and looks at us: what do you want, girls? "We'd
like some strawberries." The beautiful merchant's wife's
fingers in berry blood. Burdock, scales, basket.

Tsaritsa! The greediest woman in the world:

> *They pour foreign wines for her,*
> *She eats iced gingerbread,*
> *Terrifying guards surround her. . . .*

Once she came out of the dark shed with red hands like
that, smiling."I killed a calf . . ."

> *Axes over their shoulders. . . .*

Aargh! Let's get out of here, run, it's horrible—an icy
horror—shed, damp, death. . . .

And Uncle Pasha is the husband of this scary woman. Uncle
Pasha is small, meek, henpecked. An old man: he's fifty. He
works as an accountant in Leningrad; he gets up at five in the
morning and runs over hill and dale to make the commuter
train. Seven kilometers at a run, ninety minutes on the train,
ten minutes on the trolley, then put on black cuff protectors
and sit down on a hard yellow chair. Oilcloth-covered doors,
a smoky half-basement, weak light, safes, overhead costs—
that's Uncle Pasha's job. And when the cheerful light blue day
has rushed past, its noise done, Uncle Pasha climbs out of the

basement and runs back: the postwar clatter of trolleys, the smoky rush-hour station, coal smells, fences, beggars, baskets; the wind chases crumpled paper along the emptied platform. Wearing sandals in summer and patched felt boots in winter, Uncle Pasha hurries to his Garden, his Paradise, where evening peace comes from the lake, to the House where the huge, golden-haired Tsaritsa lies waiting on a bed with four glass legs. But we didn't see the glass legs until later. Veronika Vikentievna had been feuding a long time with Mother.

The thing was that one summer she sold Mother an egg. There was an ironclad condition: the egg had to be boiled and eaten immediately. But lighthearted Mother gave the egg to the dacha's owner. The crime was revealed. The consequences could have been monstrous: the landlady could have let her hen sit on the egg, and in its chicken ignorance it could have incubated a copy of the unique breed of chicken that ran in Veronika Vikentievna's yard. It's a good thing nothing happened. The egg was eaten. But Veronika Vikentievna could not forgive Mother's treachery. She stopped selling us strawberries and milk, and Uncle Pasha smiled guiltily as he ran past. The neighbors shut themselves in; they reinforced the wire fence on metal posts, sprinkled broken glass in strategic points, stretched barbed wire and got a scary yellow dog. Of course, that wasn't enough.

After all, couldn't Mother still climb over the fence in the dead of night, kill the dog, crawl over the glass, her stomach shredded by barbed wire and bleeding, and with weakening hands steal a runner from the rare variety of strawberries in order to graft it onto her puny ones? After all, couldn't she still run to the fence with her booty and with her last ounce of strength, groaning and gasping, toss the strawberry runner to Father hiding in the bushes, his round eyeglasses glinting in the moonlight?

From May to September, Veronika Vikentievna, who suffered from insomnia, came out into the garden at night, stood
in her long white nightgown holding a pitchfork like Nep-
tune, listening to the nocturnal birds, breathing jasmine. Of
late her hearing had grown more acute: Veronika Vikentievna
could hear Mother and Father three hundred yards away in our
dacha, with the camel's hair blanket over their heads, plotting
in a whisper to get Veronika Vikentievna: they would dig a
tunnel to the greenhouse with her early parsley.

The night moved on, and the house loomed black behind
her. Somewhere in the dark warmth, deep in the house, lost in
the bowels on their connubial bed, little Uncle Pasha lay still
as a mouse. High above his head swam the oak ceiling, and
even higher swam the garrets, trunks of expensive black coats
sleeping in mothballs, even higher the attic with pitchforks,
clumps of hay, and old magazines, and even higher the roof,
the chimney, the weather vane, the moon—across the garden,
through dreams, they swam, swaying, carrying Uncle Pasha
into the land of lost youth, the land of hopes come true, and
the chilled Veronika Vikentievna, white and heavy, would
return, stepping on his small warm feet.

Hey, wake up, Uncle Pasha! Veronika is going to die soon.

You will wander around the empty house, not a thought in
your head, and then you will straighten, blossom, look
around, remember, push away memories and desire, and
bring—to help with the housekeeping—Veronika's younger
sister, Margarita, just as pale, large, and beautiful. And in
June she'll be laughing in the bright window, bending over
the rain barrel, passing among the maples on the sunny lake.

Oh, in our declining years. . . .

But we didn't even notice, we forgot Veronika, we had
spent a winter, a whole winter, a winter of mumps and
measles, flooding and warts and a Christmas tree blazing with

tangerines, and they made a fur coat for me, and a lady in the yard touched it and said: "Mouton."

In the winter the yardmen glued golden stars onto the black sky, sprinkled ground diamonds into the connecting court-yards of the Petrograd side of town and, clambering up the frosty air ladders to our windows, prepared morning surprises: with fine brushes they painted the silver tails of firebirds.

And when everyone got sick of winter, they took it out of town in trucks, shoving the skinny snowbanks into under-ground passages protected by gratings, and smeared perfumed mush with yellow seedlings around the parks. And for several days the city was pink, stone, and noisy.

And from over there, beyond the distant horizon, laughing and rumbling, waving a motley flag, the green summer came running with ants and daisies.

Uncle Pasha got rid of the yellow dog—he put it in a trunk and sprinkled it with mothballs; he let summer renters onto the second floor—a strange, dark woman and her fat grand-daughter; and he invited kids into the house and fed them jam.

We hung on the fence and watched the strange grandmother fling open the second-story windows every hour and, illumi-nated by the harlequin rhomboids of the ancient panes, call out:

"Want milkandcookies?"

"No."

"Want potty?"

"No."

We hopped on one leg, healed scrapes with spit, buried treasures, cut worms in half with scissors, watched the old woman wash pink underpants in the lake, and found a photograph under the owner's buffet: a surprised, big-eared family with the caption, "Don't forget us. 1908."

Let's go to Uncle Pasha's. You go first. No, you. Careful, watch the sill. I can't see in the dark. Hold on to me. Will he show us *the room*. He will, but first we have to have tea.

Ornate spoons, ornate crystal holders. Cherry jam. Silly Margarita laughs in the orange light of the lamp shade. Hurry up and drink! Uncle Pasha knows, he's waiting, holding open the sacred door to Aladdin's cave. O room! O children's dreams! O Uncle Pasha, you are King Solomon! You hold the Horn of Plenty in your mighty arms. A caravan of camels passed with spectral tread through your house and dropped its Baghdad wares in the summer twilight. A waterfall of velvet, ostrich feathers of lace, a shower of porcelain, golden columns of frames, precious tables on bent legs, locked glass cases of mounds where fragile yellow glasses are entwined by black grapes, where Negroes in golden skirts hide in the deep darkness, where something bends, transparent, silvery . . . Look, a precious clock with foreign numbers and snakelike hands. And this one, with forget-me-nots. Ah, but look, look at that one! There's a glass room over the face and in it a golden Chevalier seated at a golden table, a golden sandwich in his hand. And next to him, a Lady with a goblet: and when the clock strikes, she strikes the goblet on the table—*six, seven, eight.* . . . The lilacs are jealous, they peek through the window, and Uncle Pasha sits down at the piano and plays the *Moonlight* Sonata. Who are you, Uncle Pasha?

There it is, the bed on glass legs. Semitransparent in the twilight, invisible and powerful, they raise on high the tangle of lace, the Babylon towers of pillows, the moonlit, lilac scent of the divine music. Uncle Pasha's noble white head is thrown back, a Mona Lisa smile on Margarita's golden face as she appears silently in the doorway, the lace curtains sway, the lilacs sway, the waves of dahlias sway on the slope right to the horizon, to the evening lake, to the beam of moonlight.

Play, play, Uncle Pasha! Caliph for an hour, enchanted prince, starry youth, who gave you this power over us, to enchant us, who gave you those white winds on your back, who carried your silvery head to the evening skies, crowned you with roses, illuminated you with mountain light, surrounded you with lunar wind?

> *O Milky Way, light brother*
> *Of Canaan's milky rivers,*
> *Should we swim through the starry fall*
> *To the fogs, where entwined*
> *The bodies of lovers fly?*

. . . Well, enough. Time to go home. It doesn't seem right to use the ordinary word "Thanks" with Uncle Pasha. Have to be more ornamental: "I am grateful." "It's not worthy of gratitude."

"Did you notice they have only one bed in the house?"

"Where does Margarita sleep, then? In the attic?"

"Maybe. But that's where the renters are."

"Well, then she must sleep on the porch, on a bench."

"What if they sleep in the same bed, head to foot?"

"Stupid. They're strangers."

"You're stupid. What if they're lovers?"

"But they only have lovers in France."

She's right, of course. I forgot.

. . . Life changed the slides ever faster in the magic lantern. With Mother's help we penetrated into the mirrored corners of the grownups' atelier, where the bald tubby tailor took our embarrassing measurements, muttering *excuse me's;* we envied girls in nylon stockings, with pierced ears, we drew in our textbooks: glasses on Pushkin, a mustache on Mayakovsky, a large white chest on Chekhov, who was otherwise normally endowed. And we were recognized immediately and welcomed joyfully by the patient and defective nude model from the anatomy course generously offering his numbered innards; but the poor fellow no longer excited anyone. And, looking back once, with unbelieving fingers we felt the smoked glass behind which our garden waved a hankie before going down for the last time. But we didn't feel the loss yet.

Autumn came into Uncle Pasha's house and struck him on the face. Autumn, what do you want? Wait; are you kidding? . . . The leaves fell, the days grew dark, Margarita grew stooped. The white chickens died, the turkey flew off to warmer climes, the yellow dog climbed out of the trunk and, embracing Uncle Pasha, listened to the north wind howl at night. Girls, someone, bring Uncle Pasha some India tea. How you've grown. How old you've gotten, Uncle Pasha. Your hands are spotted, your knees bent. Why do you wheeze like that? I know, I can guess: in the daytime, vaguely, and at night, clearly, you hear the clang of metal locks. The chain is wearing out.

What are you bustling about for? You want to show me your treasures? Well, all right, I have five minutes for you. It's so long since I was here! I'm getting old. So that's *it, that's* what enchanted us? All this secondhand rubbish, these chipped painted night tables, these tacky oilcloth paintings, these brocade curtains, the worn plush velvet, the darned lace, the clumsy fakes from the peasant market, the cheap beads? This sang and glittered, burned and beckoned? What mean jokes you play, life! Dust, ashes, rot. Surfacing from the magical bottom of childhood, from the warm, radiant depths, we open our chilled fist in the cold wind—and what have we brought up with us besides sand? But just a quarter century ago Uncle Pasha wound the golden clock with trembling hands. Above the face, in the glass room, the little inhabitants huddle—the Lady and the Chevalier, masters of Time. The Lady strikes the table with her goblet, and the thin ringing sound tries to break through the shell of decades. *Eight, nine, ten.* No. Excuse me, Uncle Pasha. I have to go.

. . . Uncle Pasha froze to death on the porch. He could not reach the metal ring of the door and fell face down in the snow. White snow daisies grew between his stiff fingers. The yellow dog gently closed his eyes and left through the snowflakes up the starry ladder to the black heights, carrying away the trembling living flame.

The new owner—Margarita's elderly daughter—poured Uncle Pasha's ashes into a metal can and set it on a shelf in the empty chicken house; it was too much trouble to bury him.

Bent in half by the years, her face turned to the ground, Margarita wanders through the chilled, drafty garden, as if seeking lost footsteps on the silent paths.

"You're cruel! Bury him!"

But her daughter smokes indifferently on the porch. The nights are cold. Let's turn on the lights early. And the golden Lady of Time, drinking bottoms up from the goblet of life, will strike a final midnight on the table for Uncle Pasha.

HUNTING
THE WOOLY
MAMMOTH

Zoya's a beautiful name, isn't it? Like bees buzzing by. And she's beautiful, too: a good height and all that. Details? All right, here are the details: good legs, good figure, good skin, the nose, eyes, all good. Brunette. Why not a blonde? Because you can't have everything.

When Zoya met Vladimir, he was stunned. Or well, at least pleasantly surprised.

"Oh!" said Vladimir.

That's just what he said. And wanted to see Zoya very often. But not constantly. And that saddened her.

In her one-room apartment he kept only his toothbrush—a thing that is certainly intimate, but not so much that it would

firmly tie a man to the family hearth. Zoya wanted Vladimir's
shirts, underwear, and socks to settle in, how shall we put it,
to make themselves at home in the underwear drawer, even lie
around on a chair. To be able to grab a sweater or something
and soak it, *into the Lotos soap with it,* and then dry it neatly
spread out.

But no, he didn't leave a trace; he kept everything in his
communal flat. Even his razor. Though what did he have to
shave, with that beard? He had two beards: one thick and
dark, and in the middle of it, another, smaller and reddish,
growing in a narrow tuft on his chin. A phenomenon! When
he ate or laughed, that second beard jumped. Vladimir wasn't
tall, half a head shorter than Zoya, and looked a bit wild and
hairy. And he moved very quickly.

Vladimir was an engineer.

"You're an engineer?" Zoya asked tenderly and distractedly
on their first date, when they sat in a restaurant and she opened
her lips only a millimeter to taste the profiteroles in chocolate
sauce, pretending for some intellectual reason that it wasn't
very tasty.

"Exac-tic-ally," he said, staring at her chin.

"Are you at a research institute? . . ."

"Exactically."

". . . or in industry?"

"Exactically."

Go figure him out when he was staring at her like that. And
had a bit to drink.

An engineer wasn't bad. Of course, a surgeon would have
been better. Zoya worked in a hospital, in the information
bureau, and she wore a white coat and thereby belonged a bit
to that amazing medical world, white and starched, with
syringes and test tubes, rolling carts and autoclaves, and piles
of rough, clean black-stamped laundry, and roses and tears and

chocolates, and a blue corpse rolled swiftly down endless corridors followed by a hurrying sorrowing little angel clutching to its pigeon chest a long-suffering, released soul, diapered like a doll.

And king of this world is the surgeon, who cannot be regarded without trembling as, dressed with the aid of gentlemen of the chamber in a loose-fitting mantle and green crown with laces, majestically holding his precious hands aloft, he is prepared for his holy kingly mission: to perform the highest judgment, to come down and chop off, to punish and to save, and with his glowing sword give life . . . What else, if not a king? And Zoya very much wanted to fall into a surgeon's bloody embrace. But an engineer wasn't bad.

They spent a very nice time at the restaurant, getting to know each other, and Vladimir, not realizing yet what he could count on from Zoya, was generous. It was afterward that he began to economize, looking through the menu briskly, ordering only an inexpensive main course for himself, and not lingering in restaurants. There was no need for Zoya to sit languorously with a casual expression on her face, slightly mocking, slightly dreamy—her face was supposed to reflect the fleeting nuances of her complex spiritual life, like exquisite sadness or some refined reminiscence; she ate, staring off into space, her elbows delicately resting on the table, her lower lip pouting, sending lovely smoke rings up to the painted vaulted ceiling. She was playing fairy. But Vladimir didn't play along: he ate with gusto, without a trace of sadness, gulped down his vodka, smoked without languor: quickly, greedily smelling up the table and squashing the butt in the ashtray with his yellowed finger. He brought the check close to his eyes, was horribly astounded, and always found a mistake. And he never ordered caviar: that was for princesses and thieves, he claimed. Zoya was hurt: wasn't she a princess, albeit unrecognized? And then they stopped going out completely, and stayed home. Or she stayed home alone. It was boring.

In the summer she wanted to go south to the Caucasus. There would be noise and wine and midnight swims with squeals of laughter, and masses of handsome men who would look at Zoya and say, "Oh!" and flash their teeth.

Instead, Vladimir brought a kayak to the apartment and two friends, just like him, in stinky checked shirts, and they crawled around on all fours, putting it together and taking it apart, patching, and sticking sections of the smooth repulsive kayak body in a basin of water, exclaiming: "It leaks! It doesn't leak!" while Zoya sat on the bed, jealous, annoyed by the crowding, and having to keep lifting her legs so that Vladimir could crawl from spot to spot.

Then she had to follow him and his friends on that horrible expedition to the north, to some lakes, in search of some allegedly glorious islands, and she got chilled and soaked, and Vladimir smelled of dogs. They hurried along, rowing fast, bouncing on the waves, along a grim, northern lake blown up with leaden dark waters, and Zoya sat right on the floor of the hateful kayak, legs stretched straight out, severely shortened without high heels, so pathetic and scrawny in jogging pants, and felt that her nose was red and her hair matted and the hostile spray of the water was melting her mascara, and ahead lay two more weeks of suffering in a damp tent on an uninhabited cliff covered with pine and bilberries, among offensively hearty strangers bawling cheerfully over their dinner made of pea concentrate.

And it was Zoya's turn to wash the greasy aluminum dishes in the deep icy lake, after which they were still dirty. And her hair was dirty and her head itched under her scarf.

All the engineers had their own women, no one gave Zoya special looks or said "Oh!", and she felt sexless, a camping

buddy, and she hated the laughter around the campfire, and
the guitar playing, and the peals of joy over catching a pike.
She lay in the tent totally miserable, hating the two-bearded
Vladimir, and wanted to get married to him as soon as
possible. Then she'd have the perfect right as his legal wife not
to get ugly in the so-called great outdoors, but stay home in
a light and graceful robe (full of ruffles, made in the GDR) on
the couch, legs crossed, facing a wall unit with a color TV (let
Vladimir buy her one), with pink light coming from the
Yugoslav lamp, drinking something light and smoking something good (let the patients' relatives give her some), and wait
for Vladimir to come back from his kayaking trip to greet him
a little irritated and suspicious: well, I wonder what you've
been up to without me? who was with you? did you bring any
fish? and later, of course, forgive him for his two-week
absence. And during that absence, maybe one of the surgeons
would call and flirt, and Zoya, lazily embracing the telephone
and with that look on her face, would drawl, "Oh, I don't
know . . . We'll see . . . Do you really think so?" Or she
would call a girlfriend, "So what did you say? . . . And what
did he say? And then you?" Ah, the city! Shimmer and
evenings and wet asphalt and red neon lights in the puddles
under your high heels . . .

Here the waves thudded against the cliff, and wind howled
in the tree tops, and the campfire danced its endless dance, and
night stared into your back, and the engineers' dirty-faced
ugly women squeaked in their tents. What a drag!

Vladimir adored it, got up early, while the lake was quiet
and clear, went down the steep slope, grabbing onto the pines
and getting resin on his hands, stood with his legs spread wide
on the granite shelf leading into the sunny transparent water,
washing, snorting, and groaning; looking back with happy
eyes at Zoya, sleepy, without makeup, standing grimly with a

pitcher in her hands. "Well? Have you ever heard such silence? Just listen to how quiet it is! And the air? Beautiful!" Oh, how disgusting he was! Marry him, hurry up and marry him.

In the fall Zoya bought slippers for Vladimir. Checked and cozy, they waited for him in the entrance, mouths open: slip your foot in, Vova. You're at home here, this is your snug harbor. Stay with us. Why do you keep running off, you silly fool?

Zoya stuck her photograph—chestnut curls, arched brows, severe gaze—into Vladimir's wallet: whenever he reached for his train pass or for money, he'd see her, so beautiful, and cry: ah, why aren't I marrying her? What if someone beats me to it? In the evenings, waiting for him, she placed a pink round-legged lamp in the window—a family lighthouse in the gloom. To bind the noose, to warm his heart: the tower is dark, the night is dark, but the light still burns—it is the star of his soul not sleeping, perhaps canning fruit, perhaps doing some laundry.

Soft were the pillows, soft were the dumplings put twice through the grinder, everything beckoned and Zoya buzzed like a bee: hurry, friend. Hurry up, you lousy bum!

She wanted to be married before she hit twenty-five—it was all over by then, no more youth, you get run out of the hall, and others run to take your place: swift and curly-haired.

In the mornings they drank coffee. Vladimir read *Cutters and Yachts* magazine, chewed, scattering crumbs in both beards; Zoya was hostilely silent, staring at his forehead, sending telepathic messages: marry, marry, marry, marry, marry me! In the evenings he read again, and Zoya stared out the window waiting for bedtime. Vladimir didn't read calmly, he grew excited, scratched his head, jerked his leg, laughed, and cried out, "Just listen to this!" Laughing as he spoke, jabbing Zoya with his finger, he read what he had liked so much. Zoya smiled wanly or stared at him coldly, not responding, and he would shake his head sheepishly, quiet down and mutter, "What a guy!" and out of pride keep an uncertain smile on his lips.

She knew how to spoil his fun.

But really: he had everything he wanted. Everything was swept, cleaned, the refrigerator defrosted on time. His toothbrush was here. His indoor footwear. He was fed here. If something needed to go to the cleaners—no problem. My pleasure. So what about it, you so and so, why won't you marry me and just ruin my mood? If I knew for sure that you weren't planning on it, I'd send you packing. Bye-bye. Say hi to the folks. But how to find out his intentions? Zoya didn't dare ask a direct question. Many centuries of experience kept her from doing that. One bad shot—and it was over, write it off; the prey runs away hard, leaving a cloud of dust and view of the soles of its feet. No, you have to lure it.

And the viper felt right at home. Became completely tame. Brought his shirts and jackets from the communal flat. His socks were all over the place now. He'd come over and put on the slippers. Rub his hands: "And what are we having for dinner tonight?" Notice the *we*. That's how he talked.

"Meat," Zoya said through gritted teeth.

"Meat? Fine! Fine! And why are we in a bad mood?"

Or he'd start in, "Would you like it if we got a car? We'll drive wherever we feel like."

Mockery! As if he had no plans to leave Zoya. And what if he didn't? Then marry her. Zoya didn't want to love without guarantees.

Zoya set traps: she'd dig a pit, cover it with branches, and nudge him toward it. . . . Suddenly, all dressed and made up, she would refuse to go out, lie down on the couch, and stare balefully at the ceiling. What's the matter? She can't . . .

Why? Because . . . No, what's the matter? Is she sick? What happened? She can't, she won't go, she's ashamed to be a general laughingstock, everyone will point at her: and in what capacity is this one here? Everyone else will have wives. . . . Nonsense, Vladimir would say, at best only a third will be wives there, and they'll be strangers. And Zoya had been going until now—without a problem? Until now she had, and now she can't, it's just her sensitive soul, like a rose, wilting under poor treatment.

"And when have I ever treated you poorly?"

And so on and so forth, and always moving away from the camouflaged pit.

Vladimir took Zoya to visit an artist; they say he's quite interesting. Zoya pictures the beau monde, groups of art historians: the ladies old biddies, all in turquoise and with turkey necks; the men elegant with colored handkerchiefs in their breast pockets, smelling good. A noble old man with a monocle pushes his way through the crowd. The artist in a velvet smock, pale, and with a palette in his hand. In comes Zoya. Everyone says "Oh!" The artist grows even paler. "You must pose for me." The noble old man regards her with sadness and nobility: his years are gone, Zoya's fragrant beauty is not for him. Zoya's portrait—nude—is taken to Moscow. A show at the Manege. The police hold back the crowds. There is a show abroad. The portrait is behind bulletproof glass. They let in people two at a time. Sirens wail. Everyone squeeze right. The president enters. He is astounded. Where is the original? Who is that woman? . . .

"Watch you don't break a leg down here," Vladimir said. They were going down to a basement. Mossy gunk dangled from the hot pipes. It was warm in the studio. The artist—a little snot in a torn T-shirt—dragged out his heavy paintings. They depicted strange things: for instance, a large egg, with lots of tiny people coming out of it, Mao Tse-tung in canvas boots and an embroidered jacket floating in the sky with a teapot in his hand. The whole thing was called *Concordance*. Or this one: an apple with a worm crawling out of it wearing glasses and carrying a briefcase. Or: a wild craggy cliff, growths of cattails, and from the cattails comes a wooly mammoth in slippers. Someone tiny is aiming at it with a bow and arrow. On one side you can see the little cave: it has a light bulb hanging from a cord, a glowing TV screen, and a gas burner. Even the pressure cooker is drawn in detail, and there's a bouquet of cattails on the little table. It's called *Hunting the Wooly Mammoth*. Interesting. "Well, it's daring," Vladimir said. "Quite daring. . . . What's the concept?" "Concept?" the artist gleefully demanded. "You're insulting me. Am I a Peredvizhnik or something? Concept! You have to run from concepts, brother, and don't look back!" "No, but still, but still . . ." They argued, waving their arms, the artist set out lopsided ceramic mugs on the low table, clearing not very clean space with his elbow. They drank something that didn't taste good and followed it with rock-hard pieces of the day-before-yesterday's leftovers. The host's radiant but unseeing gaze slid professionally over Zoya's surface. The gaze did not connect with Zoya's soul, as if she weren't even there. Vladimir grew red, his beards were unkempt, both men were shouting, using words like "absurd" and others that sounded like it; one referred to Giotto, the other to Moisenko, and they forgot about Zoya. She had a headache and there was a pounding in her ears: dum, dum, dum. Outside the window in the dark rain was gathering, the dusty lamp on the ceiling floated in layers of bluish smoke, and the crude white shelves were crowded with pitchers holding Crimean brambles, long broken and covered with cobwebs. Zoya wasn't here or anywhere else, she simply did not exist. The rest of the world did not exist either. Only smoke and the noise: dum, dum, dum.

On the way home, Vladimir put his arm around Zoya's shoulders.

"A most interesting man, even if he is nuts. Did you hear his arguments? Charming, eh?"

Zoya was silent and angry. It was raining.

"You're a trooper!" Vladimir went on. "Let's go home and have some strong tea, all right?"

What a louse Vladimir was. Using dishonest, cheating methods. There are rules of the hunt: the mammoth steps back a certain distance, I aim . . . let loose the arrow: *Whrrrrrrr!* and he's a goner. And I drag the carcass home: here's meat for the long winter. But this one comes on his own, gets up close, grazes, plucking at the grass, rubbing his side against the wall, napping in the sun, pretending to be tame. Allows himself to be milked! While the pen is open on all four sides. My God, I don't even have a pen. He'll get away, he will, oh Lord. I need a fence, a picket, ropes, hawsers.

Dum, dum, dum. The sun set. The sun rose. A pigeon with a banded leg landed on the window and looked severely into Zoya's eyes. There, there you are! Even a pigeon, a lousy, dirty bird gets banded. Scientists in white coats, with honest, educated faces, PhDs, pick him up, the little bird, by the sides— sorry to disturb you, fellow—and the pigeon understands, doesn't argue, and without further ado offers them his red leather foot—my pleasure, comrades. You're in the right. Click! And he flies off a different creature, he doesn't get underfoot and cry, doesn't recoil heavy-jawed out of the path of trucks, no—now he flies scientifically from cornice to balcony, intellectually consumes the prescribed grains and remembers firmly that even the gray splotches of his droppings are illuminated henceforth with the unbribable rays of science: the

Academy knows, is in control, and—if necessary—will ask.

She stopped talking to Vladimir, sat and stared out the window, thinking for hours about the scientific pigeon. Feeling the engineer's sorrowful eye upon her, she would concentrate: well? Where are the long-awaited words? Say it! Give up?

"Zoya dear, what's the matter. I treat you with love, and you treat me like a . . ." mumbled Mr. Two-Beards.

Her features hardened and sharpened, and no one has said "Oh!" in a long time upon meeting her, and she didn't need that anymore: the blue flame of endless sorrow, burning in her soul, put out all the fires of the world. She didn't feel like doing anything, and Vladimir vacuumed, beat the rugs, canned eggplant "caviar" for the winter.

Dum, dum, dum beat in Zoya's head, and the pigeon with the fiery wedding ring rose from the dark, his eyes stern and reproachful. Zoya lay down on the couch straight and flat, covered her head with the blanket, and put her arms along her sides. *Unbounded Grief,* that's what the medieval masters from the album on the shelf on the left would have called her wooden sculpture. *Unbounded Grief;* so there. Oh, they would have sculpted her soul, her pain, all the folds of her blanket the right way, they would have sculpted her and then fixed it up on tippy top of a dizzying, lacy cathedral, at the very top, and the photo would be in close up: "*Zoya.* Detail. Early Gothic." The blue flame heated the woolen cave, there was no air. The engineer was tiptoeing out of the room. "Where are you going?" Zoya shouted like a crane, and the married pigeon grinned. "I was . . . just going to . . . wash up. . . . You rest," the monster whispered fearfully.

"First he goes to wash up, then to the kitchen, and the front door is right there," the pigeon whispered in her ear. "And then he's gone."

He was right. She tossed a noose around the two-beards' neck, lay down, jerked, and listened. At that end there was rustling, sighing, shuffling. She had never particularly liked this man. No, let's be honest, he had always repulsed her. A small, powerful, heavy, quick, hairy, insensitive animal.

It puttered around for a while—whimpering, fussing—until it quieted down in the blissful thick silence of the great ice age.

THE
CIRCLE

The world is ended, the world is distorted, the world is closed, and it is closed around Vassily Mikhailovich.

At sixty, fur coats get heavy, stairs grow steep, and your heart is with you day and night. You've walked and walked, from hill to hill, past shimmering lakes, past radiant islands, white birds overhead, speckled snakes underfoot, and you've arrived here, and this is where you've ended up; it's dark and lonely here, and your collar chokes you and your blood creaks in your veins. This is sixty.

This is it, it's over. Here no grass grows. The soil is frozen, the earth is narrow and stony, and ahead only one sign glows: exit.

But Vassily Mikhailovich was not willing.

He sat in the hallway of the beauty shop and waited for his wife. Through the open door he could see the crowded room, partitioned with mirrors, where three . . . three women his own age squirmed in the hands of mighty blond furies. Could he call what was multiplying in the mirrors "ladies"? With growing horror, Vassily Mikhailovich peered at what sat closest to him. A curly-haired siren planted her feet firmly, grabbed *it* by the head, pulled it back onto a waiting metal sink, and splashed it with boiling water: steam rose; she lathered wildly; more steam, and before Vassily Mikhailovich could cry out she had fallen upon her victim and was choking it with a white terry towel. He looked away. In another chair—my God—long wires were attached to a reddened, albeit very happy head, with protruding diodes, triodes, and resistors. . . . In the third chair, he realized, was Yevgeniya Ivanovna, and he went over to her. What at home appeared to be her hair was now wrinkled up, revealing her scalp, and a woman in a white coat was dabbing at it with a stick dipped in a liquid. The odor was stifling.

"Take off your coat!" several voices cried.

"Zhenya, I'm going for a walk, just a quick circle," Vassily Mikhailovich said, waving his arm. He had felt weak in the legs since morning, his heart was thumping and he was thirsty.

In the lobby stiff green sabers grew hilt-down out of large pots, and photographs of bizarre creatures with not-so-nice hints in their eyes stared from the walls under incredible hair—towers, icing, rams' horns; or, ripples like mashed potatoes in fancy restaurants. And Yevgeniya Ivanovna wanted to be one of them.

A cold wind blew, and small dry flakes fell from the sky. The day was dark, empty, brief; its evening had been born with the dawn. Lights burned brightly and cozily in the small stores. A tiny, glowing, sweet-smelling store, a box of miracles, had grown onto the corner. You couldn't get in: people were pushing and shoving, reaching over heads with their chits, grabbing little somethings. A fat woman was trapped in the doorway, she clutched the jamb, she was being carried away by the flow.

"Let me out! Let me get out!"

"What's in there?"

"Lip gloss!"

Vassily Mikhailovich joined the jostling. *Woman, woman, do you exist? . . . What are you? . . .* High up a Siberian tree your hat blinks its eyes in fear; a cow gives birth in suffering so you can have shoes; a lamb is sheared screaming so you can warm yourself with its fleece; a sperm whale is in its death throes; a crocodile weeps; a doomed leopard pants, fleeing. Your pink cheeks come from boxes of flying dust, your smiles from golden containers with strawberry filling, your smooth skin from tubes of grease, your gaze from round transparent jars. . . . He bought Yevgeniya Ivanovna a pair of eyelashes.

. . . Everything is predestined and you can't swerve—that's what bothered Vassily Mikhailovich. You don't pick wives: they simply appear out of nowhere by your side, and you're struggling in fine netting, bound hand and foot; hobbled and gagged, you're taught thousands and thousands of stifling details of transient life, put on your knees, your wings clipped; and the darkness gathers, and sun and moon still run and run chasing each other along a circle, *the circle, the circle.*

It was revealed to Vassily Mikhailovich how to clean spoons, and the comparative physiology of meatballs and patties; he knew by heart the grievously brief lifespan of sour cream—one of his responsibilities was destroying it at the first signs of mortal agony—he knew the birthplaces of brooms and whisks,

distinguished professionally among grains, had in his head all
the prices of glassware, and every autumn wiped windowpanes
with ammonium chloride to eradicate the ice cherry orchards
that planned to grow by winter.

At times Vassily Mikhailovich imagined that he would
finish out this life and begin a new one in a new image. He
fussily selected his age, an era, his looks: sometimes he wanted
to be born a fiery southern youth; or a medieval alchemist; or
the daughter of a millionaire; or a widow's beloved cat; or a
Persian king. Vassily Mikhailovich calculated, compared,
deliberated, made conditions, grew ambitious, rejected all
suggested possibilities, demanded guarantees, huffed, grew
tired, lost his train of thought; and, leaning back in his
armchair, stared long and hard in the mirror at himself—the
one and only.

Nothing happened. Vassily Mikhailovich was not visited by
a six-winged seraph or any other feathery creature with offers
of supernatural services; nothing burst open, there was no
voice from the heavens, no one tempted him, carried him
aloft, or hurled him down. The three-dimensionality of existence, whose finale was ever approaching, suffocated Vassily
Mikhailovich; he tried to get off the tracks, drill a hole in the
sky, leave through a drawing of a door. Once, dropping off
sheets at the laundry, Vassily Mikhailovich stared into the
blossoming clover of cotton expanses, and noticed that the
seven-digit notation sewn onto the northeast resembled a
telephone number; he secretly called, and was graciously
welcomed, and began a boring joyless affair with a woman
named Klara. Klara's house was just like Vassily Mikhailovich's, with the same clean kitchen, although the windows
faced north, and the same cot, and as he got into Klara's
starched bed Vassily Mikhailovich saw yet another telephone
number in the corner of the pillow case; he doubted that his

fate awaited him there, but, bored by Klara, he called and found the woman Svetlana with her nine-year-old son; in Svetlana's linen closet, clean folded linen lay with pieces of good soap in between the layers.

Yevgeniya Ivanovna sensed that something was up, looked for clues, rummaged in his pockets, unfolded scraps of paper, unaware that she was sleeping in the pages of a large telephone book with Klara's telephone number, or that Klara dreamed in Svetlana's telephone numbers, or that Svetlana reposed, as it turned out, in the number of the accounting department of the social security office.

Vassily Mikhailovich's women never did learn of one another's existence; but of course, Vassily Mikhailovich did not pester them with information about himself. And where would he have gotten a surname, a job, an address, or say, a zip code—he, the phantom of blanket covers and pillow cases, born of the whims of chance of the laundry office?

Vassily Mikhailovich stopped the experiment, not because of the social security office; it was just that he realized that the attempt to escape the system of coordinates was a failure. It wasn't a new, unheard-of road with breathtaking possibilities that opened before him, not a secret path into the beyond, no; he had simply felt around in the dark and grabbed the usual wheel of fate and if he went around it hand over hand, along the curve, along the circle, he would eventually end up with himself, from the other side.

For, after all, somewhere in the bustling crowd, in the thick tangle of back streets, a nameless old woman was tossing a sack of worn linen marked with a seven-digit cryptogram into a small wooden window: you were enciphered in it, Vassily Mikhailovich. In all fairness, you belong to the old woman. She has every right to you—what if she makes her demand? You don't want that? Vassily Mikhailovich—*no, no, no*—

didn't want a strange old woman, he was afraid of her stockings, and her feet, and her yeasty smell, and the creak of bedsprings under her white elderly body, and he was sure she'd have a tea mushroom growing in a three-liter jar—a slippery eyeless silent creature, living years very quietly on the windowsill without splashing even once.

But the one who holds the thread of fate in his hands, who determines meetings, who sends algebraic travelers from Point A to Point B, who fills pools from two pipes, had already marked with a red X the intersections where he was to meet Isolde. Now, of course, it was quite some time since she had passed away.

He saw Isolde at the market and followed her. A peek from the side at her face blue with cold, at her transparent grapelike eyes, and he knew: she would be the one to bring him out of the tight pencil case called the universe. She wore a shabby fur coat with a belt and a thin knit hat—those caps were offered by the dozens by the stocky, heavy women who blocked the entrances to the market; women who like suicides are banned within the gates, turned away from proper stalls, and whose shadows, hard in the frost, wander in crowds along the blue fence, holding in their outstretched hands piles of wooly pancakes—raspberry, green, canary, rustling in the wind— while the early November flakes fall, fall, blowing and whistling, hurrying to wrap the city in winter.

And Vassily Mikhailovich, his heart contracting with hope, watched the meek Isolde, chilled to the bone, to an icy crunch, wander through the black crowd and drop inside the gates and run her finger along the long, empty counters, looking to see if there was anything tasty left.

The northern blizzards had blown away the hothouse sellers of capricious summer produce, those sweet marvels created on high by warm air from pink and white flowers. But the last faithful servants of the soil stood firm, frozen to the wooden tables, grimly offering their cold underground catch: for in the face of annual death nature gets scared, turns around, and grows head down, giving birth in the final moments to coarse, harsh, clumsy creatures—the black dome of radish, the monstrous white nerve of horseradish, the secret potato cities.

And the disappointed Isolde wandered on, along the light blue fence, past the galoshes and plywood crates, past the tattered magazines and wire brooms, past the drunkard offering white porcelain plugs, past the guy indifferently fanning out colored photographs; past and past, sad and shivering, and a pushy woman was already spinning right before her blue face, and praising, and scratching a bright woolen wheel, tugging at it with a big-toothed metal brush.

Vassily Mikhailovich took Isolde by the arm and offered her some wine, and his words glistened with winy sparkle. He led her to a restaurant and the crowd parted for them, and the coat check took her raiments as if they were the magical swan feathers of a fairy bather who had come from the heavens to a small forest lake. The columns emitted a soft marble aroma, and roses floated in the dim lighting. Vassily Mikhailovich was almost young, and Isolde was like a wild silvery bird, one of a kind.

Yevgeniya Ivanovna sensed Isolde's shadow, and she dug pits, put up barbed wire, and forged chains to keep Vassily Mikhailovich from leaving. Lying next to Yevgeniya Ivanovna with his heart pounding, he saw with his inner eye the cool calm of fresh snow glowing on the midnight streets. The untouched whiteness stretched, stretched, smoothly turned the corner: and on the corner, a Venetian window filled with pink light; and within it, Isolde lay awake listening to the unclear blizzard melody in the city, to the dark winter cellos. And Vassily Mikhailovich, gasping in the dark, mentally sent his soul to Isolde, knowing that it would reach her along the sparkling arc that connected them across the city, invisible to the uninitiated:

> *Night trains jangle in my throat,*
> *It comes, and grabs, and grows silent once more.*
> *The crucified hangs above a deep hole*
> *Where angels of death buzz like gnats:*
> *"Give up! You're locked in a square,*
> *We'll come, release you, and start over once more."*
> *O woman! Apple tree! Candle flame!*
> *Break through, chase away, protect, scream!*
> *Hands tied, mouth contorted,*
> *A black maiden sings in the dark.*

Vassily Mikhailovich chewed through the chain and ran away from Yevgeniya Ivanovna; he and Isolde sat holding hands, and he flung open wide the doors to his soul's treasures. He was as generous as Ali Baba, and she was astonished and trembled. Isolde did not ask for anything: not a crystal toilette, not the queen of Sheba's colored sash; she would be happy to sit forever at his side, burning like a wedding candle, burning without extinguishing with a steady quiet flame.

Soon Vassily Mikhailovich had told her everything he had to tell. Now it was Isolde's turn: she had to wrap her weak blue arms around him and step with him into a new dimension, so that lightning, with a flash, would shatter the ordinary world like an eggshell. But nothing of the kind happened. Isolde just trembled and trembled, and Vassily Mikhailovich was bored. "Well, Lyalya?" he would say with a yawn.

He paced the room in his socks, scratched his head, smoked by the window, and stuck the butts in the flower pots, packed his razor in his suitcase: he planned to go back to Yevgeniya Ivanovna. The clock ticked, Isolde cried, not understanding,

promising to die, there was slush beneath the window. Why
make a scene? Why didn't she grind some meat and make
patties instead? I said I was leaving, that meant I was leaving.
What was unclear about that?

Yevgeniya Ivanovna was so glad she baked a carrot pie,
washed her hair, polished the floors. He celebrated his fortieth
birthday first at home, then in a restaurant. They packed the
uneaten fish and jellied meat in plastic bags, and there was
enough for lunch the next day. He got good presents: a radio,
a clock with a wooden eagle, and a camera. Yevgeniya
Ivanovna had been dreaming of being photographed at the
beach in the surf. Isolde did not control herself and sort of
ruined the party. She sent some stuff wrapped in paper and an
unsigned poem, in her childish handwriting:

> *Here is a gift for you in parting:*
> *Candle stub,*
> *Shoe laces and a plum pit.*
> *Look closely and smile crookedly.*
> *This was*
> *Your love until it died:*
> *Fire, and skipping, and sweet fruit*
> *Above the abyss, and the brink of disaster.*

She was no longer alive.

And now he was sixty, and the wind blew up his sleeves,
into his heart, and his legs refused to go. Nothing, nothing
was happening, nothing lay ahead, and really there was
nothing behind, either. For sixty years he'd been waiting for
them to come and call him and show him the mystery of
mysteries, for red dawn to blaze over half the world, for a
staircase of rays to rise from earth to heaven and archangels
with trombones and saxophones or whatever they used to blare
their unearthly voices to welcome the chosen one. But why

were they taking so long? He'd been waiting his whole life.

He hastened his step. While they shaved Yevgeniya Ivanovna's neck, boiled her head, and bent her hair with metal hooks, he could reach the market and have some warm beer. It was cold, his fur coat was cheap, a fur coat in name only—fake leather lined with fake fur—which Yevgeniya Ivanovna bought from a speculator. "She skins crocodiles for herself, though," thought Vassily Mikhailovich. They had gone to the speculator—for crocodile shoes, the fur coat, and other trifles—in the evening, searching a long time for the right house. It was dark on the landing, they felt around, having no matches. Vassily Mikhailovich swore softly. To his amazement he felt a peephole at knee level on one of the doors.

"That's the right place, then," his wife whispered.

"What does she do, crawl around on all fours?"

"She's a dwarf, a circus midget."

With bated breath he felt the nearness of a miracle: beyond the vinyl-covered door, perhaps the one and only door in the world, gaped the passageway into another universe, breathed living darkness, and a tiny, translucent elf soared among the stars, trembling on dragonfly wings, tinkling like a bell.

The dwarf turned out to be old, mad, mean, and didn't let them touch any of the things. Vassily Mikhailovich surreptitiously looked at the bed with the stepladder, the children's chairs, the photographs hung low, just above the floor, testimony to the faded charms of the lilliputian. There, in the pictures, standing on the back of a dolled-up horse, in ballet togs, in glass circus diamonds, happy, tiny, the young speculator waved through the glass, through time, through a lifetime. And here, pulling enormous adult clothing out of the closet with tiny wrinkled hands, the evil troll ran back and forth, the guardian of underground gold, and the Gulliver shadow cast by the low-hanging lamp also ran back and forth.

Yevgeniya Ivanovna bought the fur coat, and the crocodile
shoes, and a winking Japanese wallet, and a scarf with Lurex
threads, and an arctic fox skin for a hat from the horrible child,
and while they made their way down the dark stairs, support-
ing each other, she explained to Vassily Mikhailovich that you
clean arctic fox with farina grains heated in a dry skillet, and
that the skin side of the fur should be kept away from water,
and that she now had to buy a half meter of plain ribbon.
Vassily Mikhailovich, trying not to remember any of this,
thought about what the dwarf had been like in her youth, and
whether dwarfs can marry, and that if they were to jail her for
speculation, the prison cell would seem so big and frightening
to her, every rat would be like a horse, and then he imagined
that the young speculator was imprisoned in a gloomy barred
castle with nothing but owls and bats: she wrung her doll-like
hands, it was dark and he was creeping toward the castle with
a rope ladder over his shoulder through the evil grounds; only
the moon ran behind the black branches like a silver apple, and
the dwarf clutched the bars of her window and squeezed
through, transparent as a lollipop in the moonlight, and he
climbed up, tearing his fingers on the mossy medieval stones,
and the guards were asleep leaning on their halberds, and a
raven steed pawed the ground below ready to gallop around
the sawdust arena, on the red carpet, around and around the
circle.

The time allotted to Vassily Mikhailovich was running out.
The ocean was behind him, but the unexplored continent had
not blocked his path, new lands had not floated out of the
mist, and with depression he could make out the dreary palms
and familiar minarets of India, which the miscalculating
Columbus had thirsted for and which meant the end of the
road for Vassily Mikhailovich. The trip around the world was
coming to an end: his caravel, having circled life, was sailing

up from the other side and was entering familiar territory. The familiar social security office, where the pensions fluttered on flag poles, hove into view, then the opera house, where Svetlana's son, wearing stage eyebrows, sang about the ephemerality of life to the loud applause of Yevgeniya Ivanovna.

"If I run into Isolde," Vassily Mikhailovich made a bet with fate, "my path is over." But he was cheating: Isolde had passed away a long time ago.

Sometimes he still got signals: you are not alone. There are clear meadows in the groves of people, where in hermits' cabins live the ascetics, the chosen who reject the bustle, who seek the secret loophole out of prison.

News arrived: strange objects were appearing, at first glance insignificant, useless, but imbued with a secret meaning; indicators leading to nowhere. One was Cheburashka, a daring challenge to school Darwinism, an old shaggy evolutionary link that fell out of the measured chain of natural selection. Another was Rubik's cube, a breakable, changeable, but always whole hexahedron. Having stood four hours in the cold along with thousands of grim fellow sect members, Vassily Mikhailovich became the owner of the marvelous cube and spent weeks twisting and twisting its creaking movable facets, until his eyes grew red, waiting in vain for the light to another universe to shine at last from the window. But sensing one night that of the two of them, the real master was the cube, which was doing whatever it wanted to with helpless Vassily Mikhailovich, he got up, went to the kitchen, and chopped up the monster with a cleaver.

In anticipation of revelation he leafed through typewritten pages that taught you to breathe a green square in through one nostril at dawn and to chase it with mental power up and down your intestines. He spent hours standing on his head with his legs crossed in someone's apartment near the railroad station,

between two unshaven, also upside-down engineers, and the
rumble of the trains outside the house speeding into the
distance shook their upraised striped socks. And it was all in
vain.

Ahead was the market, spattered with booths. Twilight,
twilight. Illuminated from inside were the icy windows of the
booth where winter sells a snowy pulp covered with chocolate
on a splintery stick and the colorful gingerbread house where
you can buy various kinds of poisonous smoke and a folding
spoon and chains of special very cheap gold; and the desired
window where a group of black figures huddled, hearts
warmed by happiness, and where a beery dawn glowed
translucently with wandering flames in the thick glass of
mugs. Vassily Mikhailovich got in line and looked around the
snowy square.

There was Isolde, legs spread apart. She was blowing beer
foam onto her cloth boots, horrible-looking, with a cracked
drunken skull and red wrinkled face. Lights were coming on
and the first stars were rising: white, blue, green. The icy
wind came from the stars to the earth, stirring her uncovered
hair, and after circling around her head, moved on to the dark
doorways.

"Lyalya," said Vassily Mikhailovich.

But she was laughing with new friends, stumbling, holding
up her mug: a big man was opening a bottle, another man
struck the edge of the counter with a dried fish, they were
having a good time.

"My heart sings with joy," Isolde sang. "Oh, if I could feel
this way forever."

Vassily Mikhailovich stood and listened to her sing without
understanding the words and when he came to, a struggling
Isolde was being led away by the militiamen. But that
couldn't be Isolde: she had passed away a long time ago.

And he, it seemed, was still alive. But now there was no point to it. Darkness pressed against his heart. The hour of departure had struck. He looked back one last time and saw only a long cold tunnel with icy walls, and himself, crawling with a hand extended, grimly smothering all the sparks that flashed on the way. The queue shoved him and hurried him, and he took a step forward, no longer feeling his legs, and he gratefully accepted from gentle hands his well-earned cup of hemlock.

A CLEAN
SHEET

His wife fell asleep the minute she lay down on the couch in the nursery: nothing wears you out as much as a sick child. Good, let her sleep there. Ignatiev covered her with a light blanket, stood around, looked at her open mouth, exhausted face, the black roots of her hair—she had stopped pretending to be a blonde a long time ago—felt sorry for her, for the wan, white, and sweaty Valerik, for himself, left, went to bed, and lay without sleep, staring at the ceiling.

Depression came to Ignatiev every night. Heavy, confusing, with lowered head, it sat on the edge of the bed and took his hand—a sad sitter for a hopeless patient. And they spent hours in silence, holding hands.

The house rustled at night, shuddered, lived. There were peaks in the vague din—a dog's bark, a snatch of music, the thud of the elevator going up and down on a thread—the night boat. Hand in hand with depression Ignatiev said nothing: locked in his heart, gardens, seas, and cities tumbled; Ignatiev was their master, they were born with him, and with him they were doomed to dissolve into nonbeing. My poor world, your master has been conquered by depression. Inhabitants, color the sky in twilight, sit on the stone thresholds of abandoned houses, drop your hands, lower your heads: your good king is ill. Lepers, walk the deserted streets, ring your brass bells, carry the bad tidings: brothers, depression is coming to the cities. The hearths are abandoned and the ashes are cold and grass is growing between the slabs where the bazaar once was boisterous. Soon the low red moon will rise in the inky sky, and the first wolf will come out of the ruins, raise its head and howl, sending a lone call on high, into the icy expanses, to the distant blue wolves sitting on branches in the black groves of alien universes.

Ignatiev did not know how to cry, and so he smoked. The light glowed in tiny toy flashes of summer lightning. Ignatiev lay there, depressed, tasting tobacco bitterness and knowing that in it was truth. Bitterness, smoke, a tiny oasis of light in the dark—that was the world. On the other side of the wall the plumbing rumbled. His earthy, tired, dear wife slept under a torn blanket. White Valerik was restless—thin, sickly shoot, pathetic to the point of spasms—rash, glands, dark circles under his eyes. And somewhere in the city, in one of the brightly lit windows, unfaithful, unsteady, evasive Anastasia was drinking wine with someone else. Look at me . . . but she just laughs and looks away.

Ignatiev turned on his side. Depression moved closer to him and flung up her ghostly sleeve—a line of ships floated up. The sailors were drinking with the locals in taverns, the captain stayed late on the governor's veranda (cigars, liqueurs, pet parrot), the watch man left his post for a cockfight and to see the bearded woman at the motley sideshow; the painters quietly untied themselves, a night breeze came up, and the old sailing ships, creaking, left the harbor for points unknown. Sick children, small, trusting boys, sleep soundly in their berths; they snuffle, holding a toy tight in their fists; the blankets slip off, the empty decks sway, the flock of ships sails with a soft splash into the impenetrable dark, and the pointed wake smooths out on the warm black surface.

Depression waves a sleeve and spreads out a boundless stony desert—hoarfrost shining on the cold rocky plain, stars frozen indifferently, the white moon indifferently drawing circles, the steadily stepping camel's bridle jangling sadly, a rider drawing near, wrapped in chilled striped cloth of Bukhara. Who are you, rider? Why have you dropped your reins? Why have you wrapped up your face? Let me loosen your stiff fingers. What is this, rider, are you dead? . . . The rider's mouth gapes, a bottomless pit; his hair is tangled, and deep sorrowful gutters have been etched in his cheeks by tears flowing for millennia.

A flutter of the sleeve. Anastasia, floating lights over a swamp. What was that slurp in the thicket? Don't look back. A hot flower beckons you to step on the springy brown hummocks. A thin, impatient fog moves about, sometimes lying down, sometimes hanging over the kindly beckoning moss: the red flower floats, winking through the white clumps: *come here, come here.* One step—that's not scary, is it? One more step—you're not afraid, are you? Shaggy heads stand in the moss, smiling, winking. A noisy dawn. Don't be afraid, the sun won't rise. Don't be afraid, we still have the fog. Step. Step. Step. Floating, laughing, the flower flashes.

Don't look back! I think I'll get it. I *do* think I'll get it. I will. *Step.*

"Oo-oo-oo," came a groan from the next room. Ignatiev pushed through the door in a bound and rushed to the crib—what's the matter, what is it? His tangled wife jumped up and they began jerking at Valerik's sheets and blanket, getting in each other's way. Just to do something, to act! The little white head tossed and turned in its sleep, muttered, *ba-da-da, ba-da-da.* Rapidly muttering, pushing them away with his hands; then he calmed down, turned, settled down. . . . He went off into his dreams alone, without his mother, without me, down the narrow path under the pines.

"What's the matter with him?"

"Another fever. I'll sleep here."

"I've already brought you a blanket. I'll get you a pillow."

"He'll be like that till morning. Shut the door. If you want to eat, there are some cheese pastries."

"I'm not hungry. Get some sleep."

Depression was waiting, lying in the wide bed; moved over, made room for Ignatiev, embraced him, put her head on his chest, on the razed gardens, the dried-up seas, the ashen cities.

But not everything was killed: toward morning, when Ignatiev slept, Life came out of the dugouts; it pulled apart the burned logs and planted small seedlings: plastic primroses, cardboard oaks; hauled building blocks to erect temporary shelter, filled the seas with a watering can, cut pink bug-eyed crabs out of oilcloth, and with an ordinary pencil drew the dark, convoluted line of the surf.

After work, Ignatiev did not go straight home, but drank beer with a friend in a little cellar bar. He always hurried to get the

best spot, in the corner, but rarely succeeded. And while he
hurried, avoiding puddles, speeding up, patiently waiting for
the roaring rivers of cars to pass, behind him, shuffled into the
crowd of people, depression hurried; here and there, her flat,
dull head appeared. There was no way he could get away from
her, the doorman let her into the cellar bar, too, and Ignatiev
was happy if his friend also came early. Old friend, schoolmate:
he waved to him from afar, nodding, smiling gaptoothed; his
thinning hair curled over his old, worn jacket. His children
were grown. His wife had left him a long time ago and he
didn't want to remarry. Everything was just the opposite with
Ignatiev. They met joyously and parted irritated, unhappy
with each other, but the next time they started all over again.
And when his friend, panting, made his way through the
arguing tables, and nodded to Ignatiev, then deep in Ignatiev's chest, in his solar plexus, Life raised its head and also
nodded and waved.

They ordered beer and pretzels.

"I'm in despair," Ignatiev said. "I'm desperate. I'm confused. It's all so complicated. My wife is a saint. She quit her
job, she spends all her time with Valerik. He's sick, he's sick
all the time. His legs don't work well. He's just this tiny little
candle stump. Barely burning. The doctors give him shots,
he's afraid. He screams. I can't stand hearing him scream. The
most important thing for him is home care and she kills
herself. She's killing herself. But I can't go home. Depression.
My wife won't even look me in the eye. And what's the point?
Even if I read *The Old Man and the Turnip* to Valerik at
bedtime, it's still depressing. And it's a lie; if a turnip is stuck
in the ground, you can't get it out. I know. Anastasia. . . . I
call and call, she's never home. And if she is home, what can
we talk about? Valerik? Work? . . . It's bad, you know, it
gets me down. Every day I promise myself: tomorrow I'll wake

up a new man, I'll perk up, I'll forget Anastasia, make a
pile of money, take Valerik down south. . . . Redo the
apartment, start jogging in the morning . . . But at night,
I'm depressed."

"I don't understand," his friend would say. "What are you
making this into such a big deal for? We all live pretty much
the same way, what's the problem? We all manage to live
somehow."

"You don't understand. Right here"—Ignatiev pointed to
his chest—"it's alive, and it hurts."

"You're such a fool," his friend said and picked his teeth
with a wooden match. "It hurts because it's alive. What did
you expect?"

"I expected it not to hurt. It's too hard for me. Believe it or
not, I'm suffering. And my wife is suffering, and so is Valerik,
and Anastasia must be suffering and that's why she unplugs
the phone. And we all torment one another."

"You're a fool. Just don't suffer."

"I can't."

"You're a fool. Big deal, the world-class sufferer! You just
don't want to be hale and hearty, you don't want to be master
of your life."

"I'm at the end of my tether," Ignatiev said, clutching his
hair and staring at his foam-flecked mug.

"You're an old woman. You're wallowing in your self-
invented suffering."

"No, I'm not an old woman. And I'm not wallowing. I'm
sick and I want to be well."

"If that's the case, you should know: the diseased organ has
to be amputated. Like an appendix."

Ignatiev looked up, shocked.

"What do you mean?"

"I just told you."

"Amputated in what sense?"

"Medically. They do that now."

His friend looked around, lowered his voice, and explained: there's an institute near Novoslobodskaya, and they operate on it; of course, it's still semiofficial for now, it's done privately, but it's possible. Of course, you have to make it worth the surgeon's while. People come out completely renewed. Hadn't Ignatiev heard about it? It's very widespread in the West, but it's still underground here. Has to be done on the sly. Bureaucracy.

Ignatiev listened, stunned.

"But have they at least . . . experimented on dogs?"

His friend made circles near his ear.

"You're really nuts. Dogs don't have it. They have reflexes. Remember Pavlov?"

"Oh, yes."

Ignatiev thought a bit. "But it's horrible!"

"There's nothing horrible about it. The results are excellent: the mental processes become much sharper. Will power increases. All those idiotic, fruitless doubts end forever. Harmony of body and, uh, brain. The intellect beams like a projector. You set your goal, strike without missing, and grab first prize. But I'm not forcing you, you know. If you don't want treatment, stay sick. With your glum nose. And let your women unplug the phone."

Ignatiev did not take offense, he shook his head: those women . . .

"Ignatiev, for your information, what you tell a woman, even if she's Sophia Loren, is: shoo! Then they'll respect you. Otherwise, you don't count."

"But how can I say that to her? I worship her, I tremble . . ."

"Right. Tremble. You tremble, I'm going home."

"Wait! Stay a bit. Let's have another beer. Listen, have you seen any of these . . . *operated* people?"

"You bet."

"How do they look?"

"How? Like you and me. Better. Everything's just dandy with them, they're successful, they laugh at fools like us. I have a pal, we were at college together. He's become a big shot."

"Could I have a look at him?"

"A look? Well, all right, I'll ask. I don't know if he'd mind. I'll ask. Although, what's it to him? I don't think he'll refuse. Big deal!"

"What's his name?"

"N."

It was pouring. Ignatiev walked through the city in the evening; red and green lights replaced each other, bubbling on the streets. Ignatiev had two kopeks in his hand, to call Anastasia. A Zhiguli drove right through a puddle on purpose, splashing Ignatiev with murky water, splattering his trousers. Things like that happened frequently to Ignatiev. "Don't worry, I'll get that operation," thought Ignatiev, "buy a car, and I'll splash others. Revenge on the indifferent for humiliation." He was ashamed of his base thoughts and shook his head. I'm really sick.

He had a long wait at the phone booth. First a young man whispered smiling into the phone. Somebody whispered back a long time, too. The man ahead of Ignatiev, a short, dark man, banged his coin against the glass: have a heart. Then he called. Apparently he had his own Anastasia, but her name was Raisa. The short man wanted to marry her, insisted, shouted, pressed his forehead against the cold telephone.

"What's the problem?" He couldn't understand. "Can you please explain what the problem is? What more could you want? Tell me! Just tell me! You'll be rolling . . ."—he switched the receiver to his other ear—"You'll be rolling in clover! Go on. Go on." He listened a long time, tapping his foot. "Why my whole apartment is covered with rugs. Yeah. Yeah." He listened a long time, grew bewildered, stared at the phone with its dial tone, left with an angry face, with tears in his eyes, walked into the rain. He didn't need Ignatiev's sympathetic smile. Ignatiev crawled into the warm inside of the booth, dialed the magical number, but crawled out with nothing: his long rings found no response, dissolved in the cold rain, in the cold city, beneath the low, cold clouds. And Life whimpered in his chest until morning.

N. received him the next week. A respectable establishment with lots of name plates. Solid, spacious corridors, carpets. A weeping woman came out of his office. Ignatiev and his friend pushed the heavy door. N. was an important man: desk, jacket, the works. Just look, look! A gold pen in his pocket, and look at the pens in the granite slab on his desk. Look at the desk calendars. And a fine cognac behind the square panes of his cupboard—well, well!

His friend explained their visit. He was visibly nervous: even though they had been at college together, all those pens . . . N. was clear and precise. Get all possible analyses. Chest X rays—profile and frontal. Get transferred to the institute by your local hospital, without making a fuss, put the reason: For *tests*. And at the institute, go to Dr. Ivanov. Yes, Ivanov. Have one hundred fifty rubles ready in an envelope. That's basically it. That's what I did. There may be other ways, I don't know.

Yes, quick and painless. I'm satisfied.

"So, they cut it out?"

"I'd say, tear it out. Extract it. Clean, hygienic."

"And afterward . . . did you see it? After the extraction?"

"What for?"

N. was insulted. Ignatiev's friend kicked him: indecent questions!

"Well, to know what it was like," Ignatiev said embarrassedly. "You know, just . . ."

"Who could possibly be interested in that? Excuse me . . ." N. lifted the edge of his cuff: a massive gold timepiece was revealed. With an expensive strap. Did you see, did you notice? The audience was over.

"Well, what did you think?" His friend peered into his face as they walked along the embankment. "Are you convinced? What do you think?"

"I don't know yet. It's scary."

Headlights splashed in the black river waves. Depression, his evening girlfriend, was creeping up on him. Peeking out from behind the rain gutter pipe, running across the wet pavement, blending into the crowd, watching constantly, waiting for Ignatiev to be alone. Windows were lighting up, one after another.

"You're in bad shape, Ignatiev. Decide. It's worth it."

"I'm scared. This way I feel bad, the other way I'm scared. I keep thinking, what happens later? What comes after? Death?"

"Life, Ignatiev! Life! A healthy, superior life, not just chicken scratching. A career. Success. Sport. Women. Get rid of complexes and neuroses! Just look at yourself: what are you? A wimp. Coward! Be a man, Ignatiev! A man! That's what women want. Otherwise, what are you? Just a rag!"

Yes, women. Ignatiev drew Anastasia and grew lonely. He remembered her last summer, leaning toward a mirror,

radiant, plump, her reddish hair tossed back, putting on
carrot-colored lipstick, her lips in a convenient cosmetic
position, talking in spurts, with pauses.

"I doubt. That you're. A man. Ignatiev. Because men. Are.
Decisive. And-by-the-way-change-that-shirt-if-you-have-any-
hopes-at-all." And her red dress burned like a flower.

And Ignatiev was ashamed of his tea-colored short-sleeved
silk shirt, which used to belong to his father. It was a good
shirt, long-wearing; he had gotten married in it and had
welcomed Valerik home from the hospital in it. But if a shirt
stands between us and the woman we love, we'll burn the
shirt—even if it's made of diamonds. And he burned it. And
it helped for a short while. And Anastasia loved him. But now
she was drinking red wine with others and laughing in one of
the lit windows of this enormous city, he didn't know which
one, but he looked for her silhouette in each one. And—not to
him, but to others, shifting her shoulders under the lace
shawl, on the second, seventh, sixteenth floor—she was saying
her shameless words: "Am I really *very* pretty?"

Ignatiev burned his father's tea-colored shirt; its ashes fall
on the bed at night, depression sprinkles him with it, softly
sowing it through half-shut fist. Only the weak regret useless
sacrifices. He will be strong. He will burn everything that
erects obstacles. He'll grow into the saddle, he'll tame the
evasive, slippery Anastasia. He will lift the claylike, lowered
face of his beloved, exhausted wife. Contradictions won't tear
him apart. The benefits will balance clearly and justly. Here is
your place, wife. Reign. Here is your place, Anastasia. Rule.
And you: smile, little Valerik. Your legs will grow strong and
your glands will stop swelling, for Papa loves you, you pale
city potato seedling. Papa will be rich, with pens. He will call
in expensive doctors in gold-rimmed glasses with leather cases.
Carefully handing you from one to the other, they will carry

you to the fruity shores of the eternally blue sea, and the lemony, orangey breeze will blow the dark circles away from your eyes. Who's that coming, tall as a cedar, strong as steel, with his step springy, knowing no shameful doubts? That's Ignatiev. His path is straight, his income high, his gaze confident. Women watch him pass. Shoo! . . . Down a green carpet, in a red dress, Anastasia floats toward him nodding through the fog, smiling her shameless smile.

"I'll at least get started on the paperwork. That takes ages," Ignatiev said. "And then I'll see."

Ignatiev's appointment was for eleven, but he decided to go early. A summer morning chirped outside the kitchen window. Water trucks sprayed brief coolness in rainbow fans, and Life cheeped and hopped in the tangled tree branches. Behind his back, sleepy night seeped through the netting, whispers of depression, foggy pictures of misery, the measured splash of waves on a dull deserted shore, low, low clouds. The silent ceremony of breakfast took place on a corner of the oilcloth—an old ritual whose meaning is forgotten, purpose lost; what remains is only the mechanical motions, signs, and sacred formulas of a lost tongue no longer understood by the priests themselves. His wife's exhausted face was lowered. Time had long since stolen the pink flush of youth from the thousand-year-old cheeks and their branched fissures. . . . Ignatiev raised his hand, cupped it, to caress the parchment tresses of the beloved mummy—but his hand encountered only the sarcophagus' cold. Frozen cliffs, the jangle of a lone camel's bridle, the lake, frozen solid. She did not lift her face, did not lift her eyes. The mummy's wrinkled brown stomach: dried up, sunken, the sliced-open rib cage filled with balsamic resins, stuffed with dry tufts of herbs; Osiris is silent. The dry members are tightly bound with linen strips marked with blue signs: asps, eagles, and crosses—the sneaky, minuscule droppings of ibis-headed Toth.

You don't know anything yet, my dear, but be patient: just a few more hours, and the shackles will burst and the glass vessel of despair will shatter into small, splashing smithereens, and a new, radiant, shining glorious Ignatiev will appear to the boom and roll of drums and the cries of Phrygian pipes, wise, intense, complete; will arrive riding on a white elephant on a rug-covered seat with colored fans. And you will stand at my right, and on my left—closer to the heart—will stand Anastasia; and white Valerik will smile and reach out, and the mighty elephant will kneel and gently swing him in his kind, ornamented trunk, and pass him to Ignatiev's strong arms, and Ignatiev will raise him above the world—the small ruler, intoxicated by heights—and the exulting nations will cry: *ecce homo! Ecce* ruler from sea to sea, from edge to edge, to the glowing cupola, the blue curving border of the gold-and-green planet earth.

Ignatiev came early, the hallway outside the office was empty, there was only a blond man hanging around, the one with the ten o'clock appointment. A pathetic blond with shifty eyes, biting his nails, nibbling his cuticle, stoop-shouldered; sitting down, then jumping up and examining closely the four-sided colored lanterns with edifying medical tales: "Unwashed Vegetables Are Dangerous." "Gleb Had a Toothache." "And the Eye Had to Be Removed" (If thine eye offend thee, pluck it out). "Give the Dysentery Patient Separate Dishes." "Air Out Your Home Frequently." An entry light went on over the door, the blond man groaned softly, patted his pockets, and crossed the threshold. Pathetic, pathetic, miserable man! I'm just like him. Time passed.

Ignatiev squirmed, sniffed the medicated air, went to look at the pedagogical lanterns; Gleb's story interested him. A sick tooth tormented Gleb, but then let up; and Gleb, cheerier, in a jogging suit, played chess with a school friend. But you can't escape your fate. Gleb suffered great torments, and bound up his face with a cloth, and his day turned to night, and he went to the wise, stern doctor, and the doctor did ease his suffering: he did pull Gleb's tooth and cast it out; and Gleb, transfigured, smiled happily in the final, bottom illuminated window, while the doctor raised his finger in admonition, bequeathing his time-honored wisdom to new generations.

Behind him came the rattle of a dolly and stifled moans, and two elderly women in white coats drove a writhing, nameless body, wrapped in dried-up bloody bandages—face and chest—only the mouth was a black hole. Could it be the blond? . . . Impossible . . . After them came a nurse with an IV, frowning, who stopped when she noticed Ignatiev's desperate signals. Ignatiev made an effort and remembered the language of humans:

"The blond?"

"What did you say? I didn't understand."

"The blond, Ivanov? . . . He had it, too? . . . Extracted it, right?"

The nurse laughed grimly.

"No, they transplanted it into him. They'll take yours out and put it in someone else. Don't worry. He's an inpatient."

"You mean they do the reverse, too? Why such . . ."

"He's doomed. They don't survive it. We make them sign a disclaimer before the surgery. It's useless. They don't live."

"Rejection? Immune system?"

"Heart attack."

"Why?"

"They can't take it. They were born that way, lived their

whole lives that way, never knowing what *it* is. And then they go and have a transplant. It must be a fad or something. There's a waiting list, we do one a month. Not enough donors."

"So, I'm a donor?"

The nurse laughed, picked up the IV, and left. Ignatiev thought. So that's how they do it here. An experimental institute, that's for sure. . . . Ivanov's office door opened, and a golden-haired someone strode out, haughty, pushy; Ignatiev jumped out of the way, then watched him go . . . the blond . . . A superman, dream, ideal, athlete, victor! The sign over the door was blinking impatiently, and Ignatiev crossed the threshold and Life rang like a bell in his trembling chest.

"Please sit for a minute."

The doctor, Professor Ivanov, was writing something on a card. They were always like that: call you in, but they're not ready. Ignatiev sat down and licked his lips. He looked around the office. A chair like a dentist's, anesthesia equipment with two silvery tanks, and manometer. Over there, a polished cupboard with small gifts from patients, harmless, innocent trifles: plastic model cars, porcelain birds. It was funny to have porcelain birds in an office where such things were done. The doctor wrote and wrote, and the uncomfortable silence thickened, the only sounds the squeal of the pen, the jangle of the lone black camel's bridle, and the stiffened rider, and the frozen plain. . . . Ignatiev squeezed his hands to control the trembling and looked around: everything was ordinary; the shutters of the old window were open and beyond the white window frame was summer.

The warm, already dusty leaves of the luxurious linden splashed, whispered, conspired about something, huddling in a tangled green mass, giggling, prompting one another, plotting: let's do it this way; or how about like this? Good idea: well, then, we're agreed, but it's our secret, right? Don't give it away! And suddenly, quivering as one heady, scented crowd, excited by the secret that united them—a wonderful, happy, warm summer secret—with a rustle, they lunged toward their neighboring, murmuring poplar: Guess, just guess. It's your turn to guess. And the poplar swayed in embarrassment, caught unawares; and muttered, recoiling: easy, easy, not all at once; calm down, I'm old, you're all so naughty. They laughed and exchanged glances, the linden's green inhabitants: we knew it! And some fell down to the ground, laughing, into the warm dust, and others clapped their hands, and still others didn't even notice, and once more they whispered, inventing a new game. Play, boys; play, girls! Laugh, kiss, live, you short-lived little green town. The summer is still dancing, its colorful flower skirts still fresh, it's only noon by the clock: the hands triumphantly pointing up. But the sentence has been read, the permission granted, the papers signed. The indifferent executioner—the north wind— has put on his white mask, packed his cold poleaxe, is ready to start. Old age, bankruptcy, destruction are inexorable. And the hour is nigh when here and there on the bare branches there will be only a handful of frozen, contorted, uncompre-hending old husks, thousand-year-old furrows on their earthy, suffering faces. . . . A gust of wind, a wave of the poleaxe, and they too will fall . . . *I don't want to, I don't want to, I don't want to, I don't want to,* thought Ignatiev. I can't hold on to summer with my weak hands, I can't stop the decay, the pyramids are collapsing, the crack has sundered my trembling heart and the horror of the witnesses' useless suffering . . . No. I'm dropping out of the game. With magic scissors I will cut the enchanted ring and go outside. The shackles will fall, the dry paper cocoon will burst, and astonished by the newness of the blue and gold purity of the world, the lightest, most fragile butterfly will fly out and grow more beautiful. . . .

Get out your scalpel, your knife, your sickle, whatever you usually use, doctor; be so kind as to sever the branch that is still blooming but is hopelessly dying and toss it in the purifying flames.

The doctor extended his hand without looking up—and Ignatiev hurried, embarrassed, afraid to do the wrong thing, handed him his pile of test results, references, X rays, and the envelope with one hundred fifty rubles—the envelope with an unseasonal Santa Claus in a painted sleigh with presents for the kiddies. Ignatiev began to look, and saw the doctor. On his head in receding cones sat a cap—a white tiara in blue stripes, a starched ziggurat. Tanned face, eyes lowered onto the papers; and falling powerfully, waterfall-like, terrifying, from his ears down to his waist, in four layers, in forty spirals: a rough, blue Assyrian beard, thick ringlets, black springs, a nocturnal hyacinth. I am Physician of Physicians, Ivanov.

"He's no Ivanov," Ignatiev thought in horror. The Assyrian picked up the Santa Claus envelope, lifted it by one corner, and asked, "What's this?" He looked up.

He had no eyes.

The empty sockets gave off the black abyss of nothingness, the underground entrance to other worlds, on the edges of the dead seas of darkness. And he had to go there.

There were no eyes, but there was a gaze. He was looking at Ignatiev.

"What is this?" the Assyrian repeated.

"Money," Ignatiev said, moving the letters.

"What for."

"I wanted to . . . they said . . . for the operation, I don't know. You take it. (Ignatiev horrified himself.) I was told, I wanted to. I was told, I asked."

"All right."

The professor opened a drawer and swept rosy-cheeked Santa with presents for Valerik into it, his tiara shifted on his head.

"Is surgical intervention indicated for you?"

Indicated? It's indicated. Isn't it indicated for everyone? I don't know. There are the test results, lots of figures, all kinds of things . . . The doctor looked down toward the papers, went through the results, good dependable results with clear purple stamps: all the projections of a cone—circle and triangle—were there; all the Pythagorean symbols, the cabalistic secrets of medicine, the backstage mysticism of the Order. The professor's clean, surgical nail went down the graphs: thrombocytes . . . erythrocytes . . . Ignatiev watched the nail jealously, mentally pushing it along: don't stop, everything is fine, good numbers, sturdy, clean, roasted nuts. Secretly proud: marvelous, healthy zeros without worms; the fours like excellently built footstools, the eights well-washed eyeglasses; everything suitable, satisfactory. Operation indicated. The Assyrian's finger stopped. What's the matter? Something wrong? Ignatiev craned his neck and looked anxiously. Doctor, is it that two over there that you don't like? Really, you're right, heh-heh, it's not quite . . . a small bruise, I agree, but it's accidental, don't pay any attention, read on, there are all those sixes over there, spilled like Armenian grapes. What, they're no good, either? . . . Wait, wait, let's figure this out. The Assyrian moved his finger and went down to the bottom of the page, then flipped through the papers, made a neat pile, and clipped it. He took out the chest X ray and held it up to the light for a long time. He added it to the pile. I think he's willing, thought Ignatiev. But anxiety blew like a draft through his heart, opening doors, moving curtains. But that too would pass. Actually, more precisely, that was exactly what would pass. I'd like to know

what it would be like after. My poor heart, your apple orchards
still stir. The bees still buzz and dig in the pink flowers,
weighed down by heavy pollen. But the evening sky is
darkening, the air is still, the shiny axe is being sharpened.
Don't be afraid. Don't look. Shut your eyes. Everything will
be fine. Everything will be fine. Everything will be very fine.

I wonder if the doctor had it done, too? Should I ask? Why
not? I'll ask. No, I'm afraid. I'm afraid and it's impolite and
maybe I'll spoil everything. If you ask, your dry tongue
moving meekly; smiling tensely, gazing beseechingly into
the nightmarish dark gaping like a black hole between his
upper and lower lids, vainly trying to meet his gaze, to find
a saving human point, find something, some sort of—well,
maybe not a welcome, not a smile, no no, I understand—but
even scorn, fastidiousness, even revulsion, *some* answer, *some*
glimmer, some sign, somebody stir, wave your hand, do you
hear me? Is anyone in there? I feel around in the dark, I feel
the dark, it's thick; I see nothing, I'm afraid I'll slip and fall,
but where can I fall if there's no path beneath my feet? I am
alone here. I am afraid. Life, are you here? . . . Doctor,
excuse me please, sorry to bother you, but just one question:
tell me, is Life there?

As if in foreboding, something in his chest cringed,
scurried, crouched, eyes shut, arms over its head. Be patient.
It will be better for everyone.

The Assyrian let him look into his deep starless pits once
more.

"Sit in the chair, please."

And I will, so what, it's no big deal, I'll just go sit,
casual-like. Ignatiev settled in the leather reclining chair.
Rubber straps on his arms and legs. On the side, a hose, tanks,
a manometer.

"General anesthesia?"

The professor was doing something at his desk, with his back to Ignatiev, and he replied reluctantly, after a pause.

"Yes, general anesthesia. We'll remove it, clean it out, fill the canal."

"Like a tooth," thought Ignatiev. He felt a cowardly chill. What unpleasant words. Easy, easy. Be a man. What's the problem. Easy. It's not a tooth. No blood. Nothing.

The doctor selected the proper tray. Something jingled on it. With tweezers he selected and placed on a low table, onto a glass medical slide, a long, thin, disgustingly thin needle, thinner than a mosquito's whine. Ignatiev squinted at it nervously. Knowing what those things were for was horrible, but not knowing was worse.

"What's that?"

"The extractor."

"So small? I wouldn't have thought."

"Do you think yours is big?" the Assyrian said irritatedly. And he stuck the X ray under his nose, but he could make out nothing but foggy spots. The doctor was already wearing rubber gloves fitted tightly over his hands and wrists, and with a bent tweezers he rummaged among the shiny bent needles and vilely narrowing probes and pulled something out: a parody of scissors with a pike's jaws. The Assyrian scratched his beard with a rubber finger. Ignatiev thought that the doctor was ruining the sterility and meekly mentioned it aloud.

"What sterility?" The professor raised his eyelids. "I wear gloves to protect my hands."

Ignatiev smiled weakly, understandingly. Of course, you never know, there are people with diseases. . . . He suddenly realized that he didn't know how they would drag it out: through his mouth? His nose? Maybe they make an incision on the chest? Or in the hole between collarbones, where day and

night the soft throb continues: sometimes hurrying, sometimes slowing its endless run?

"Doctor, how . . ."

"Quiet!" The Assyrian exclaimed. "Silence! Shut your
mouth. Just listen to me. Look at the bridge of my nose.
Count to twenty to yourself: one, two . . ."

His nose, mouth, and blue beard were firmly wrapped in
white. Between the white mask and the striped tiara the
abyss stared from his eyes. Between the two sockets, openings
into nowhere, was the bridge of his nose: a tuft of blue hairs
on a crumbling mountain range. Ignatiev began looking,
turning to ice. The anesthesia hose was moving toward him
from the side. A trunk; and from it, the sweet, sweet smell
of death. It hung over his face; Ignatiev struggled, but gave
up, tied down by rubber straps, stifled his last, too-late
doubts—and they splashed in all directions. Out of the
corner of his eye he saw depression, his loyal girlfriend,
pressed against the window, bidding him farewell, weeping,
blocking the white light, and almost voluntarily inhaled the
piercing, sweet smell of blossoming nonexistence, once,
twice, and more, without moving his eyes from the Assyrian
emptiness.

And there, in the depths of the sockets, in the otherworldly
crevasses, a light went on, a path appeared, stumps of black,
charred branches grew, and with a soft jolt Ignatiev was
sucked from the chair, forward and up, and was tossed there,
on the path, and hurrying—seven, eight, nine, ten, I'm
lost—he ran along the stones with his almost nonexistent legs.
And Life gasped behind him, and the bars clanged, and
Anastasia wailed bitterly, wildly . . .

And I'm sorry, sorry, sorry, sorry for those left behind and
I can't stop and I'm running upward, and huddled low the
dacha station flew past, and with Mama and me— a little boy,

no, it's Valerik—and they turn, mouths open, shouting; but
I can't hear them, Valerik raises his little hand, something in
his fist, the wind ruffles their hair. . . .

Ringing in the ears, darkness, ringing, oblivion.

Ignatiev—Ignatiev?—slowly floated up from the bottom, his
head pushing aside the soft, dark rags—a lake of cloth.

He lay in the chair, the straps undone, his mouth dry, his
head spinning. In his chest, a pleasant, calm warmth. It felt
good.

The bearded man in the white coat was writing something on a medical chart. Ignatiev remembered why he was
there—just a simple outpatient operation, he had to have the
whatsit removed; what was that word. The hell with it.
General anesthesia—that took pull. Not bad.

"Well, doc, can I split?" Ignatiev asked.

"Stay five minutes," the bearded one said dryly. "So pushy
all of a sudden."

"Did you do it all, no tricks?"

"All."

"Watch it, if you welshed on the deal, I'll shake my bucks
out of you real fast," Ignatiev joked.

The doctor looked up from the papers. Well, that was the
living end, a real knockout. Holes instead of eyes.

"What's the matter, pal, lose your eyeballs?" Ignatiev
laughed. He liked his new laugh—sort of a squealing bark.
Fast-like. "Well, you're really something, pal! I'm knocked
out. Just don't trip when you go pick up babes."

He liked the dull spot in his solar plexus. It was boss.

"Hey, man, I'm off. Gimme five. *Ciao*."

He slapped the doctor on the back. He bounded down the

worn stairs with sturdy, springy steps, with whiplash turns on
the landings. So much to do! And everything would work out.
Ignatiev laughed. The sun was shining. Loads of babes on the
street. Terrif. First off to Anastasia. Show her what's what!
But first, a few jokes, of course. He had made up a few jokes
already, his brain was whizzing. "Gotta keep your shotgun
clean," he'd say. He thought that up. And when he left, he'd
say, "Stay cool, suck ice." He was so funny now: no joke,
seriously, the life of the party.

Should I go home first or what? Home later, now I have to
write to the right place and tell the right people that a doctor
calling himself Ivanov takes bribes. Write it in full detail,
with a lacing of humor: he has no eyes, but all he sees is
money. Who's keeping an eye on things, anyway?

And then home. I've had it keeping that preemie home. It's
not sanitary, you know. Arrange a bed in a home for him. If
they give me trouble, I'll have to slip them something. That's
the way the game is played. It's normal.

Ignatiev pushed the post office door.

"What would you like?" the curly-haired girl asked.

"A clean sheet of paper," Ignatiev said. "Just a clean sheet."

FIRE AND DUST

I wonder where crazy Svetlana is now, the one they called Pipka, about whom some used to say with youthful fecklessness, "Pipka's not a person," and others fumed, "Why do you let her into your house? You should watch out for your books. She'll swipe them all!" They were wrong: all that lay on Pipka's conscience was the light blue Simenon and a white wool sweater with knit buttons, and that already had a mended elbow. The hell with the sweater. Much more valuable things had disappeared since then: Rimma's radiant youth, the childhood of her children, the freshness of her hopes, as pale blue as the morning sky; the secret, joyous trust with which Rimma listened to the voice of the future, whispering to her alone—she had been promised every wreath, flower, island, and rainbow, and where were they now? She didn't regret the sweater, which she herself forced on Svetlana as she pushed her out, crazy and half-dressed as usual, into the autumn fury, into the cold, branch-shaking Moscow midnight. Rimma, in her nightgown, impatiently shuffled her feet on the doorstep, lifting one foot then the other to warm them up, nodding quickly, getting out Svetlana, who kept trying to finish saying something, to tell her something, with a nervous giggle, with quick shrugs; and her black eyes burned like a mad abyss on her white, pretty face, and the wet abyss of her mouth muttered in a hurried flutter—a horrible black mouth whose tooth stubs brought an old forest fire to mind. Rimma advanced, conquering inch after inch, and Svetlana talked and talked, talked and talked, waving her arms about as if doing exercises, late-night, impossible exercises, and in describing something's enormous size—Rimma wasn't listening—she spread her arms so wide she smashed her knuckles on the wall and fell silent for a moment surprised, pressing the salty joints to her lips, to her mouth, scorched by senseless speech. It was then that the sweater was foisted on her: you'll warm up in the taxi; the door slammed, and Rimma, saddened and laughing, ran back to Fedya under the warm blanket. "Forced her out." The children turned in their sleep. They had to get up early tomorrow. "You should have let her sleep over," Fedya grumbled through his sleep, through the warmth, and he looked so handsome in the night light's glow. Sleep over? Never! And where? In old Ashkenazy's room? The old man kept tossing on his sagging couch, smoking his thick, stinking cigarettes, coughing, getting up in the middle of the night for a drink from the kitchen sink; but in general he was all right, he didn't bother her. When they had guests, he lent them chairs, brought out a jar of marinated mushrooms, pulled out a clump of sticky peppermints from a tin; placed at one end of the table, he chuckled, swinging his feet, which didn't reach the floor, and smoked into his fist: "Bear up, young people, I'll die soon and the whole apartment will be yours." "Live to be a hundred, David Danilovich," Rimma always rejoined, but it was nice to dream about the time when she would be owner of the whole apartment, her own, not a communal flat, and they would do a major remodeling, doing the awkward five-cornered kitchen in tile from floor to ceiling and putting in a new stove. Fedya would defend his dissertation, the children would go to school, English lessons, music, figure skating . . . What else could she imagine? Many of their friends already envied her her future. But, of course, it wasn't the tile nor well-rounded children that glowed from the expanses of the future in a rainbow-colored fire, a sparkling arc of delirious delight (and Rimma truly wished old Ashkenazy a long life: there was time for everything); no, something bigger, something completely different, important, exciting, and great rustled and sparkled ahead, as if Rimma's barge, sailing in a dark stream through flowering rushes, was about to be carried out into the green, joyous, roaring ocean.

And in the meantime, life wasn't completely real, it was a life of expectation, a life out of a suitcase, casual and light—with a pile of rubbish in the hallway, with midnight guests: Petyunya with the heavenly tie, childless Ella and Alyosha, and other people; with nocturnal visits from Pipka and her wild conversations. She was so horrible-looking, that Pipka, with those black stumps for teeth, but a lot of men were attracted by her, and toward the end of a party they would often be one man short: Pipka would have taken him off—always by taxi—to her place in Perlovka. She had a little wooden hut with a fence for cheap. For a while Rimma even

worried about Fedya—he was frivolous, and Pipka was crazy
and capable of anything at all. If it weren't for the rot in
Pipka's fast mouth, Rimma would have thought twice about
having her in the house. Especially since Fedya would say,
mysteriously, "If Svetlana didn't open her mouth, you could
really have a talk with her." And she was always shivering,
half-dressed, or dressed from the wrong end: children's shoes,
stiff from being soaked, on bare feet in the middle of winter,
her hands red and chapped.

No one knew what happened to Pipka, just as no one knew
where she had come from—she had just appeared, and that
was that. Her stories were wild and confused: something about
wanting to go to drama school, even being accepted; but at the
market she ran into pickled garlic vendors and was taken away,
gagged, to Baku in a white Volga without license plates.
There they violated her, knocked out half her teeth, and
abandoned her naked on the seashore in a puddle of oil; in the
morning she allegedly was found by a wild tribesman passing
through Baku, who took her to his mountain aerie and kept
her there all summer, feeding her melon from knifepoint
through a crack in the cabin wall; in the fall he traded her to
a passing ethnographer for a watch without hands. The
ethnographer, who called her Svetka-Pippetka (whence her
nickname) kept her, still naked, in an abandoned watchtower
left over from the days of Shamil, its floor laid with rotten
Persian carpets; the ethnographer studied the designs through
an eyepiece. At night eagles shat on them. "Shoo, shoo, damn
birds!" Pipka demonstrated, racing around the room with an
outraged look, frightening the children. By winter the ethnographer had moved uphill, and with the first snow Svetlana
went down into the valley, where they were still on a lunar
calendar and took potshots at teachers through the school
window and marked each death with a notch on a pole in the

middle of the marketplace. There were over eight hundred notches, the losses were not made up, and several pedagogical institutes worked to supply that valley alone. There Svetlana had an affair with the director of the local store. But she quickly ended it, considering him not manly enough: instead of sleeping like a real *djigit,* or horseman, on his back, with saber in hand and fur hat on his head, his broad shoulders spread fiercely, the director rolled up into a fetal ball, snored, whimpered, and kicked; he claimed he dreamed of gunshots. By spring, Pipka had reached Moscow, sleeping in haystacks and avoiding big roads; she was mauled by dogs several times. For some reason, she'd walked through the Urals. Geography was not her strong suit, even less so than her love life: she called the Urals the Caucasus, and she put Baku on the Black Sea. There may have been some truth in her nightmarish stories; who knows? Rimma was used to them and hardly listened, thinking her own thoughts, deep in her unhurried dreams. No one listened, really. Pipka wasn't a person, was she? Sometimes a new guest would listen to Pipka's fantasies, the fountain spewing plots, and exclaim happily and astonishedly, "Listen to her! A thousand and one nights!" It was men like that whom Pipka usually took off to her semifantastic Perlovka (if it existed at all): could you actually believe that Svetlana had been hired to dig their dahlias and ate fish meal with the chickens? As usual, in the midst of the simple fare, the din of chatter and the clink of forks, Rimma fell under a dreamy spell: glorious visions, pink and blue mists, white sails; she heard the ocean's roar, distant and beckoning, like the steady roar that came from the enormous shell that ornamented their cupboard. Rimma liked to shut her eyes and hold the shell to her ear: from the salmon-pink jaws came the call of a far land, so far away it couldn't fit on the globe; and it levitated smoothly, that country, and hung in the sky with all its lakes, parrots, and surf. And Rimma, too, soared in the sky amid the pink feathery clouds: everything that life promised would come true. She didn't have to stir, she didn't have to hurry, it would come to her. Just sail quietly in the dark stream . . . Listen to the approaching ocean's roar. . . . Rimma opened her eyes and looked, smiling, through the tobacco smoke and the dreams at her guests, at indolent, satisfied Fedya, at David Danilovich dangling his legs, and slowly came down to earth. It would start with something small . . . It would start slowly . . .

With legs woozy from her flight, she felt for the floor. Oh, first: the apartment. The old man's room would be the bedroom. Blue curtains. No, white. White, silk, luxuriant, gathered. And a white bed. Sunday morning. Rimma in a white peignoir, with loosened hair (she'd have to start growing her hair, but she had already bought the peignoir secretly: couldn't resist) would walk to the kitchen. Coffee aroma . . . She would tell new acquaintances, "And in the room where our bedroom is, a little old man used to live: so sweet, he never bothered us. And after his death we moved in. So sad; such a marvelous old man."

Rimma swayed in her chair, smiling at the still-alive old man: "You smoke too much, David Danilovich. You should take better care of yourself." The old man merely coughed and waved his hand: what's the difference. Haven't got long to go. So what.

How pleasant to sail and soar through time—but time soars through you and melts behind you, and the ocean's roar still beckons: we ought to go south and breathe the sea air and stand on the shore, arms outspread, and listen to the wind; how sweetly life melts—the children, and loving Fedya, and the anticipation of the white bedroom. The guests envy me; yes, go ahead my dears and envy, for enormous happiness awaits me, I won't tell you what, I don't know myself, but voices whisper: wait, wait! Here's Petyunya sitting and envying and chewing his nails. He doesn't have a wife or an apartment, he's skinny and vain, he wants to be a journalist, he loves bright ties; we should give him ours, the orange one; we don't need it, happiness awaits us. Here are Ella and Alyosha; they're envious too, they don't have children, they've gotten a dog, what a bore. There's old Ashkenazy, envying my youth, my white bedroom, my ocean's roar; good-bye old man, you have to leave soon, eyes squinting under copper coins. Here's Svetlana: she doesn't envy anyone, she has everything, except it's imaginary, her eyes and her horrible mouth blaze like a fire—move Fedya away from her, she's babbling wildly, dozens of kingdoms rise and fall in her mind in the course of a single evening. Move Fedya away. Fedya! Come sit here. She's lying again, and you believe it?

It was fun and easy living, teasing Petyunya and his passion for ties, predicting a great journalistic future for him, asking him not to forget them when he started traveling abroad; Petyunya would get embarrassed and wrinkle up his sweet face: come on, guys, I'll be lucky to graduate. Petyunya was a sweetie, but somehow weak; and yet he tried to flirt with Rimma, though of course rather obliquely: he cut onions for her in the kitchen and hinted that he had, to tell the truth, fantastic plans. Rimma laughed: what plans, when she had great expectations herself? Why don't you make a play for Ella, she's going to leave Alyosha anyway. Or how about Svetka-Pippetka. Pippetka's getting married, Petyunya said. To whom, I'd like to know?

Soon they knew to whom: to old Ashkenazy. The old man, pitying Pipka's feet in children's shoes and her frozen hands, sorry about her extravagant expenses for nighttime taxis, giving in to a general geriatric generosity, decided—behind

Rimma's back—to marry the black-fire-breathing tramp and to register her, naturally, for the living space promised to Rimma and Fedya. There was a row with heart medicine. "Shame on you! Shame on you!" shouted Rimma in a broken voice. "I have nothing to be ashamed about," the old man replied from the couch, lying down amid the rusted springs, with his head back to stop his nosebleed. Rimma put cold compresses on him and spent the night by his side. When he fell asleep, breathing lightly and unevenly, she measured the window in his room. Yes, the white fabric was wide enough. Blue wallpaper would be good. In the morning they made up, Rimma forgave the old man, he wept; she gave him Fedya's shirt and made hot cakes. Svetlana learned something was up and did not come by for a long time. Then Petyunya disappeared too, and they assumed that Svetlana had taken him off to Perlovka. Anyone who ended up there would be gone for a long time and would take a while to get back to normal upon returning.

Petyunya came back six months later, one evening, with a bewildered stare, and clay-smeared trousers. Rimma had trouble prying a word out of him. Yes, he had been there. He'd helped Pipka with the work. Very hard life. Everything was very complicated. He had walked from Perlovka. Why the clay? Oh, that. . . Last night he and Pipka had wandered around Perlovka with a kerosene lamp, looking for a house. A Circassian there had a puppy. Yes, that's what I said. Yes, I know—Petyunya pressed his hands to his chest—I know there are no Circassians in Perlovka. He's the last one. Svetlana said she knew it for a fact. It would be a great story for the newspaper, for the "Just the Facts" column.

"Are you crazy, too?" Rimma asked, blinking.

"Why do you say that? I saw the puppy with my own eyes."

"What about the Circassian?"

"They wouldn't let us in. It was late."

"Sleep it off," said Rimma. She put him to bed in the hallway, among the clutter. Rimma tossed and turned all night and by morning had decided that Circassian was a dog's name. But at breakfast she didn't want to add to the delirium with questions, and anyway Petyunya was grim and left quickly.

Then Svetlana had to move all her things from Perlovka to some other place—there was no point in trying to get the geography straight—by taxi, naturally, and for some reason she had to have Fedya's help. After some hesitation, Rimma let him go. It was ten in the morning, what could possibly . . . He came back at three the next morning, in a strange state.

"Where were you?" Rimma was waiting for him in her nightgown in the corridor.

"You see, there's lots of circumstances. . . . We had to go to Serpukhov, her twins are in the orphanage there."

"What twins?" shouted Rimma.

"Tiny, only a year or so. Siamese twins. Their heads are joined together. Karina and Angela."

"What heads? Are you crazy? She's been coming to our house for a hundred years, have you seen her have a baby?" No, of course he hadn't seen her have a baby or anything like it, but they did go to Serpukhov, they brought a nice parcel: a frozen fish. Yes, a fish for the twins. He paid for it himself. Rimma burst into tears and slammed the door; Fedya was left in the corridor, scratching at the door and swearing he didn't understand a thing himself, but he definitely remembered Karina and Angela.

Pipka disappeared for a long time after that, and the episode was forgotten. But something snapped in Rimma for the first time; she looked back and saw that time was still flowing but the future wasn't coming any closer, and Fedya wasn't so handsome anymore and the children had already picked up bad words on the street, and old Ashkenazy kept coughing and living and she had wrinkles around her eyes and mouth, and the rubbish was still in the corridor. And the ocean's roar was dimmer and they never did go south, they kept putting it off for the future that didn't want to come.

Troubled days followed. Rimma gave up. She kept trying to find out when she'd missed the path leading to the distant singing happiness, and often sat lost in thought while the children grew, while Fedya sat by the TV and didn't want to write his dissertation, while a cottony blizzard howled outside or the saccharine urban sun peeked through summer clouds. Their friends aged, became sticks in the mud, Petyunya vanished completely; bright ties went out of fashion, Ella and Alyosha got a new bratty dog whom no one would take care of in the evenings. At the office, Rimma had new coworkers, Big Lusya and Little Lusya, but they didn't know of Rimma's plans for happiness and didn't envy her; instead they envied Kira from the planning section who dressed expensively, traded hats for books, books for meat, meat for medicine or tickets to hard-to-get plays, and told someone irritatedly over the phone, "But you know perfectly well how much I like tongue in aspic."

And one evening, as Fedya sat in front of the TV and Rimma sat with her head on the table listening to the old man cough in the next room, Pipka burst in, all fire and flame, with pink cheeks, younger, as often happens with the mad, and smiling with a blazing mouth filled with sparkling white teeth.

"Thirty-six!" she shouted from the door, and struck her fist on the sash.

"Thirty-six *what?*" asked Rimma, lifting her head from the table.

"Thirty-six teeth!" said Pipka. And told them she had signed on as a cabin boy on a ship going to Japan; and since the ship was overstaffed, she had to sleep in the vats with the meat and rice; the captain saluted her and his assistant slept with her, and en route a rich Japanese man fell in love with her and wanted to get married by cable, without putting it off, but they didn't have the right hieroglyphs or something and that fell through; and then, while they were in port washing out the vats for the meat and rice, she was kidnapped by a pirate junk and sold to a rich plantation owner, and she worked on a Malaysian hemp plantation from where she was bought by a rich Englishman for a Soviet special anniversary-issue ruble— as you know, highly prized by Malaysian numismatists—and the Englishman took her off to foggy Albion, lost her at first in the thick fog, but then found her and in great joy paid for the most expensive and fashionable selection of thirty-six teeth, which only a moneybags can do. He gave her some smoked pony meat for the road, and now she was finally going to Perlovka for her things.

"Open your mouth," Rimma said hostilely. And in Svetlana's mouth, readily opened, she counted, fighting off dizziness, all thirty-six: how they all fit was unclear, but they really were teeth.

"I can bite through a steel cable now; if you want, I'll bite off the cornice," the monster began, and Fedya looked up with great interest, but Rimma waved her arms: enough, enough, it's late, we're sleepy; and gave her money for a taxi and pushed her to the door and handed her a volume of Simenon: please, you can read it at bedtime, just go! And Pipka left, clutching at the walls in vain, and no one ever saw her again.

"Fedya, will we go south?" Rimma asked.

"Of course," Fedya replied readily, as he had so many times over the years. Good. So, we'll really go. South! And she listened to the voice which still whispered, barely audibly, about the future, about happiness, about deep long sleep in the white bedroom; but the words were hard to make out now.

"Hey, look! It's Petyunya!" Fedya said in amazement. On the TV screen, underneath palm trees, small and grim, with a microphone in his hands, stood Petyunya criticizing a cocoa plantation owner, while passing blacks turned to look at him and his huge tie boiled up with the African dawn; but he didn't look so happy, either.

Now Rimma knew that they had all been tricked; but who had done it and when, she couldn't remember. She went over every day, looking for the mistake, but couldn't find it. Everything was covered with a layer of dust. Sometimes she wanted—strange—to talk about it with Pipka, but she never came back.

It was summer again, it was hot, and through the thick dust the voice from the future began whispering. Rimma's children were grown, one married and the other in the army, the apartment was empty and she didn't sleep well at night: the old man coughed ceaselessly. Rimma no longer wanted to turn the old man's room into a bedroom, and the white peignoir was gone: eaten by a moth that came out of the rubbish in the corridor, that didn't even see what it ate.

At work, Rimma complained to Big Lusya and Little Lusya that the moths were even eating German clothes; the little one gasped with her hands on her cheeks, and the big one grew angry.

"If you want to restock, girls," said experienced Kira, tearing herself away from her phone machinations, "I can take you to a place. I have a woman. Her daughter just got back from Syria. You can pay later. Good stuff. Vera Esafovna bought seven hundred rubles' worth on Saturday. They lived well in Syria. Swam in a pool, they want to go again."

"Let's go, all right," said Big Lusya.

"Oooh, I have so many debts as it is," whispered the little one.

"Hurry, hurry, girls, let's take a cab," Kira rushed them. "We'll manage during lunch hour." Feeling like schoolgirls playing hooky, they piled into a cab, filling it with perfume and lit cigarettes, and raced down the hot summer side streets sprinkled with sunny linden blossoms and splotches of warm shade; a southern wind blew and brought through the gasoline fumes the triumph and radiance of the distant south: the blue blaze of the skies, the mirrored sparkle of the enormous seas, wild happiness, wild freedom, the madness of hopes coming true—for what? Who knows? And in the apartment which they entered meekly, anticipating a happy garment adventure, there was also a warm wind, moving and billowing the white netting on the windows and the doors opening on the spacious balcony. Everything here was spacious, large, free. Rimma envied the apartment. A mighty woman—the owner of the items on sale—quickly flung open the door to the desired room. The goods were piled, crumpled, into TV cartons and onto the double bed, reflected in the mirror of the mighty wardrobe.

"Rummage away," Kira said, taking charge from the doorway. Trembling, the women plunged their hands into the boxes of silks, velvets, diaphanous gold-embroidered things; they pulled them out, tugging, getting tangled in ribbons and ruffles; their hands fished out one thing while their eyes were already on another, enticed by a bow or trim, and inside Rimma a tiny vein throbbed; her ears burned, and her mouth was dry. It was like a dream. And, as the cruel scenario of a dream demanded, she quickly noticed a break in the harmony developing fast, a secret defect threatening to turn into a catastrophe. The things—what *was* this?—were wrong, not the ones they had first appeared to be; her eye could discern the silliness of those flashy gauze cotton skirts, good only for the *corps de ballet,* the pretentiousness of the purple turkey-cock jabots, the unfashionable lines of the heavy velvet jackets. These were rejects: we were invited for leftovers from some-body's banquet; others had rummaged here; someone's greedy hands had defiled the magic boxes, torn out and taken away the real things that made my heart pound and that special vein throb. Rimma attacked other boxes, picked through the jumble on the double bed, but there . . . and there . . . The things she pulled desperately out of the piles and held up against herself, looking anxiously into the mirror, were ridiculously small, short, or dumb. Life had passed by, and the voice of the future sang for others. The owner of the goods sat like a Buddha and watched them closely and scornfully.

"How about that?" Rimma pointed at things on hangers along the walls, swaying in the warm wind.

"Sold. That's sold, too."

"What about something in my size?"

"Why don't you give her something," Kira said, leaning against a wall. The woman thought, and then pulled out something gray from behind her back; and Rimma, stripping quickly, revealing the secrets of her cheap underwear to her friends, squeezed like an eel into the appropriate openings; smoothing and tugging, she looked into her mercilessly bright reflection. The warm wind wandered through the sunny room, indifferent to the business at hand. She didn't really see what she was trying on, she looked with depression at her white legs with black hairs, that seemed as if they were mildewed, or had been in a trunk all winter, at her frightened, extended neck with its goose flesh, at her sticky hair, her stomach, her wrinkles, the dark circles under her eyes. The dress smelled of someone else—it had been tried on.

"Very good. It's *you*. Take it," Kira urged, the woman's secret ally. The woman watched silently and scornfully.

"How much?"

"Two hundred." Rimma suffocated, trying to pull off the poisoned garment.

"It's very fashionable, Rimmochka," Little Lusya said guiltily. And to complete the humiliation, the wind blew open the door to the next room and revealed a heavenly vision: the woman's young, divinely slim, nut-brown daughter—the one who had lived in Syria, who had swum in white pools in transparent blue water: a flash of a white dress, blue eyes. The woman rose and shut the door. Not a sight for mere mortals.

The southern wind carried linden droppings into the old courtyard and warned the worn walls. Little Lusya sidled down the steps, holding a mountain of clothes, almost weeping—more horrible debts. Big Lusya kept an angry silence. Rimma also went down with clenched jaw: the summer day had darkened, fate had teased her and laughed. And she already knew that the blouse she bought at the last moment in a spurt of desperation was garbage, last year's leaves, fool's gold that would turn black in the morning, a shell sucked and spat out by the blue-eyed Syrian houri.

She rode in the quiet, sad taxi, and told herself: at least I have Fedya and the children. But the solace was artificial and meager, for everything was over, life was showing its empty face: hair askew and gaping eye sockets. And the dreamed-of south, where she had wanted to go for so many years, now seemed yellow and dusty, with tufts of scrubby dry grasses, with murky unrefreshing waves, with bobbing expectorations and scraps of paper. And at home there was the smelly old, communal flat, and immortal old Ashkenazy, and familiar Fedya, so familiar she could scream, and the whole viscous flow of the future years—as yet unlived, but already known—

through which she had to plod and plod as if through dust
covering the path up to her knees, her waist, her neck. And
the siren song deceptively whispering sweet words of what
would not be to the stupid swimmer fell silent forever.

Oh, there were still a few events: Kira's arm shriveled up,
Petyunya came to visit and spoke at length about oil prices,
Ella and Alyosha buried their dog and got a new one, old
Ashkenazy finally washed his windows with the help of the
Zarya cleaning service: but Pipka never showed up. Some were
certain she'd married a blind fortune-teller and moved to
Australia—to flash her new white teeth among the eucalyptus
and platypuses over the coral reefs: while others swore that she
was killed and burned in a taxi on the Yaroslavl Highway on
a rainy, slippery night, and that the flames were visible a long
way off, a pillar reaching to the skies. They also said that they
hadn't been able to put out the flames, and when the fire had
burned itself out, they found nothing at the site of the
accident. Just some lumps of charcoal.

DATE
WITH A
BIRD

"Boys! Dinner time!"

The boys, up to their elbows in sand, looked up and came back to the real world: their mother was on the wooden porch, waving; this way, come on, come on! From the door came the smells of warmth, light, an evening at home.

Really, it was already dark. The damp sand was cold on their knees. Sand castles, ditches, tunnels—everything had blurred into impenetrability, indistinguishability, formlessness. You couldn't tell where the path was, where the damp growths of nettles were, where the rain barrel was . . . But in the west, there was still dim light. And low over the garden, rustling the crowns of the dark

wooded hills, rushed a convulsive, sorrowful sigh: that was
the day, dying.

Petya quickly felt around for the heavy metal cars—cranes,
trucks; Mother was tapping her foot impatiently, holding the
doorknob, and little Lenechka had already made a scene, but
they swooped him up, dragged him in, washed him, and
wiped his struggling face with a sturdy terry towel.

Peace and quiet in the circle of light on the white
tablecloth. On saucers, fans of cheese, of sausage, wheels of
lemon as if a small yellow bicycle had been broken; ruby lights
twinkled in the jam.

Petya was given a large bowl of rice porridge; a melting
island of butter floated in the sticky Sargasso Sea. Go under,
buttery Atlantis. No one is saved. White palaces with emerald
scaly roofs, stepped temples with tall doorways covered with
streaming curtains of peacock feathers, enormous golden
statues, marble staircases going deep into the sea, sharp silver
obelisks with inscriptions in an unknown tongue—everything,
everything vanished under water. The transparent green ocean
waves were licking the projections of the temples; tanned,
crazed people scurried to and fro, children wept. . . . Looters
hauled precious trunks made of aromatic wood and dropped
them; a whirlwind of flying clothing spread. . . . Nothing
will be of use, nothing will help, no one will be saved,
everything will slip, list, into the warm, transparent
waves. . . . The gold eight-story statue of the main god, with
a third eye in his forehead, sways, and looks sadly to the
east. . . .

"Stop playing with your food!"

Petya shuddered and stirred in the butter. Uncle Borya,
Mother's brother—we don't like him—looks unhappy; he has
a black beard and a cigarette in his white teeth; he smokes,
having moved his chair closer to the door, open a crack into

the corridor. He keeps bugging, nagging, mocking—what does he want?

"Hurry up kids, straight to bed. Leonid is falling asleep."

And really, Lenechka's nose is in his porridge, and he's dragging his spoon slowly through the viscous mush. But Petya has no intention of going to bed. If Uncle Borya wants to smoke freely, let him go outside. And stop interrogating him.

Petya ate doomed Atlantis and scraped the ocean clean with his spoon, and then stuck his lips into his cup of tea—buttery slicks floated on the surface. Mother took away sleeping Lenechka, Uncle Borya got more comfortable and smoked openly. The smoke from him was disgusting, heavy. Tamila always smoked something aromatic. Uncle Borya read Petya's thoughts and started probing.

"You've been visiting your dubious friend again?"

Yes, again. Tamila wasn't dubious, she was an enchanted beauty with a magical name, she lived on a light blue glass mountain with impenetrable walls, so high up you could see the whole world, as far as the four posts with the signs: South, East, North, West. But she was stolen by a red dragon who flew all over the world with her and brought her here, to this colony of summer dachas. And now she lived in the farthest house, in an enormous room with a veranda filled with tubs of climbing Chinese roses and piled with old books, boxes, chests, and candlesticks; smoked thin cigarettes in a long cigarette holder with jangling copper rings, drank something from small shot glasses, rocked in her chair, and laughed as if she were crying. And in memory of the dragon, Tamila wore a black shiny robe with wide sleeves and a mean red dragon on the back. And her long tangled hair reached down to the armrests of the chair. When Petya grew up he would marry Tamila and lock Uncle Borya in a high tower. But later—maybe—he would have mercy, and let him out.

Uncle Borya read Petya's mind again, laughed, and sang—
for no one in particular, but insulting anyway.

> *A-a-ana was a seamstress,*
> *And she did embroidery.*
> *Then she went on sta-age*
> *And became an actress!*
> *Tarum-pam-pam!*
> *Tarum-pam-pam!*

No, he wouldn't let him out of the tower.

Mother came back to the table.

"Were you feeding Grandfather?" Uncle Borya sucked his
tooth as if nothing were wrong.

Petya's grandfather was sick in bed in the back room,
breathing hard, looking out the low window, depressed.

"He's not hungry," Mother said.

"He's not long for this world," Uncle Borya said, and
sucked his tooth. And then he whistled that sleazy tune again:
tarum-pam-pam!

Petya said thank you, made sure the matchbox with his
treasure was still in his pocket, and went to bed—to feel sorry
for his grandfather and to think about his life. No one was
allowed to speak badly of Tamila. No one understood anything.

. . . Petya was playing ball at the far dacha, which went
down to the lake. Jasmine and lilacs had grown so luxuriantly
that you couldn't find the gate. The ball flew over the bushes
and disappeared in the garden. Petya climbed over the fence
and through the bushes—and found a flower garden with a
sundial in the center, a spacious veranda, and on it, Tamila.
She was rocking in a black rocker, in the bright-black robe,
legs crossed, pouring herself a drink from a black bottle; her
eyelids were black and heavy and her mouth was red.

"Hi!" Tamila shouted and laughed as if she were crying. "I was waiting for you."

The ball lay at her feet, next to her flower-embroidered slippers. She was rocking back and forth, back and forth, and blue smoke rose from her jangling cigarette holder, and there was ash on her robe.

"I was waiting for you," Tamila repeated. "Can you break the spell on me? No? Oh dear . . . I thought . . . Well, come get your ball."

Petya wanted to stand there and look at her and hear what she would say next.

"What are you drinking?" he asked.

"*Panacea,*" Tamila said, and drank some more. "Medicine for all evil and suffering, earthly and heavenly, for evening doubts, for nocturnal enemies. Do you like lemons?"

Petya thought and said: I do.

"Well, when you eat lemons, save the pits for me, all right? If you collect one hundred thousand pits and make them into a necklace, you can fly even higher than the trees, did you know that? If you want, we can fly together, I'll show you a place where there's buried treasure—but I forgot the word to open it up. Maybe we'll think of it together."

Petya didn't know whether to believe her or not, but he wanted to keep looking at her, to watch her speak, watch her rock in that crazy chair, watch the copper rings jangle. She wasn't teasing him, slyly watching his eyes to check: Well? This is interesting, isn't it? Do you like it? She simply rocked and jangled, black and long, and consulted with Petya, and he understood: she would be his friend ages unto ages.

He came closer to look at the amazing rings shining on her hand. A snake with a blue eye circled her finger three times; next to it squatted a squashed silver toad. Tamila took off the snake and let him look at it, but she wouldn't let him see the toad.

"Oh no, oh no; if you take that off, it's the end of me. I'll turn into black dust and the wind will scatter me. It protects me. I'm seven thousand years old, didn't you know?"

It's true, she's seven thousand years old, but she should go on living, she shouldn't take off the ring. She's seen so much. She saw Atlantis perish—as she flew over the doomed world wearing her lemon-pit necklace. They had wanted to burn her at the stake for witchcraft, they were dragging her when she struggled free and soared up to the clouds: why else have the necklace? But then a dragon kidnapped her, carried her away from her glass mountain, from the glass palace, and the necklace was still there, hanging from her mirror.

"Do you want to marry me?"

Petya blushed and replied: I do.

"That's settled. Just don't let me down! We'll ratify our union with a word of honor and some chocolates."

And she handed him a whole dish of candies. That's all she ate. And drank from that black bottle.

"Want to look at the books? They're piled over there."

Petya went over to the dusty mound and opened a book at random. It was a color picture: like a page from a book, but he couldn't read the letters, and on top in the corner there was a big colored letter, all entwined with flat ribbon, grasses, and bells, and above that a creature, half-bird, half-woman.

"What's that?" Petya asked.

"Who knows. They're not mine," Tamila said, rocking, jangling, and exhaling.

"Why is the bird like that?"

"Let me see. Ah, that bird. That's the Sirin, the bird of death. Watch out for it: it will choke you. Have you heard somebody wailing, cuckooing in the woods at night? That's this bird. It's a night bird. There's also the Finist. It used to fly to me often, but then we had a fight. And there's another bird, the Alkonost. It gets up in the morning at dawn, all pink and transparent, you can see through it, and it sparkles. It makes its nest in water lilies. It lays one egg, very rare. Do you know why people pick lilies? They're looking for the egg. Whoever finds it will feel a sense of longing all their life. But they still look for it, they still want it. Why, *I* have it. Would you like it?"

Tamila rocked once on the black bentwood rocker and went into the house. A beaded cushion fell from the seat. Petya touched it; it was cool. Tamila came back, and in her hand, jingling against the inside of her rings, was the magical egg, pink glass, tightly stuffed with golden sparkles.

"You're not afraid? Hold it! Well, come visit me." She laughed and fell into the rocker, moving the sweet, aromatic air.

Petya didn't know what it was to be depressed for life, and took the egg.

Definitely, he would marry her. He had planned to marry his mother, but now that he had promised Tamila . . . He would definitely take his mother with him, too; and if it came to that, he could take Lenechka, as well . . . but Uncle Borya—no way. He loved his mother very, very much, but you'd never hear such strange and marvelous stories as Tamila's from her. Eat and wash up—that was her whole conversation. And what they bought; onions or fish or something.

And she'd never even heard of the Alkonost bird. Better not tell her. And he'd put the egg in a matchbox and not show it to anybody.

Petya lay in bed and thought about how he would live with Tamila in the big room with the Chinese roses. He would sit on the veranda steps and whittle sticks for a sailboat he'd call *The Flying Dutchman.* Tamila would rock in her chair, drink the panacea, and talk. Then they would board *The Flying Dutchman,* the dragon flag on the mast, Tamila in her black

robe on the deck, sunshine and salt spray, and they would set
sail in search of Atlantis, lost in the shimmering briny deep.

He used to live a simple life: whittling, digging in the
sand, reading adventure books; lying in bed, he would listen
to the night trees anxiously moving outside his window, and
think that miracles happened on distant islands, in parrot-
filled jungles, or in tiny South America, narrowing downward,
with its plastic Indians and rubber crocodiles. But the world,
it turned out, was imbued with mystery, sadness, and magic,
rustling in the branches, swaying in the dark waters. In the
evenings, he and his mother walked along the lake: the sun set
in the crenellated forest, the air smelled of blueberries and pine
resin, and high above the ground red fir cones glimmered
gold. The water in the lake looks cold, but when you put your
hand in, it's even hot. A large gray lady in a cream dress walks
along the high shore: she walks slowly, using a stick, smiles
gently, but her eyes are dark and her gaze empty. Many years
ago her little daughter drowned in the lake, and she is waiting
for her to come home: it's bedtime, but the daughter still
hasn't come. The gray lady stops and asks, "What time is it?"
When she hears the reply, she shakes her head. "Just think."
And when you come back, she'll stop and ask again, "What
time is it?"

Petya has felt sorry for the lady ever since he learned her
secret. But Tamila says little girls don't drown, they simply
cannot drown. Children have gills: when they get underwater
they turn into fish, though not right away. The girl is
swimming around, a silver fish, and she pokes her head out,
wanting to call to her mother. But she has no voice . . .

And here, not far away, is a boarded-up dacha. No one
comes to live there, the porch is rotted through, the shutters
nailed, the paths overgrown. Evil had been done in that dacha,
and now no one can live there. The owners tried to get tenants,

even offered them money to live there; but no, no one will. Some people tried, but they didn't last three days: the lights went out by themselves, the water wouldn't come to a boil in the kettle, wet laundry wouldn't dry, knives dulled on their own, and the children couldn't shut their eyes at night, sitting up like white columns in their beds.

And on that side—see? You can't go there, it's a dark fir forest; twilight, smoothly swept paths, white fields with intoxicating flowers. And that's where the bird Sirin lives, amid the branches, the bird of death, as big as a wood grouse. Petya's grandfather is afraid of the bird Sirin, it might sit on his chest and suffocate him. It has six toes on each foot, leathery, cold, and muscular, and a face like a sleeping girl's. *Cu-goo! Cu-goo!* the Sirin bird cries in the evenings, fluttering in its fir grove. Don't let it near Grandfather, shut the windows and doors, light the lamp, let's read out loud. But Grandfather is afraid, he watches the window anxiously, breathes heavily, plucks at his blanket. *Cu-goo! Cu-goo!* What do you want from us, bird? Leave Grandfather alone! Grandfather, don't look at the window like that, what do you see there? Those are just fir branches waving in the dark, it's just the wind acting up, unable to fall asleep. Grandfather, we're all here. The lamp is on and the tablecloth is white and I've cut out a boat, and Lenechka has drawn a rooster. Grandfather?

"Go on, go on, children." Mother shoos them from Grandfather's room, frowning, with tears in her eyes. Black oxygen pillows lie on a chair in the corner—to chase away the Sirin bird. All night it flies over the house, scratching at windows; and toward morning it finds a crack, climbs up, heavy, on the windowsill, on the bed, walks on the blanket, looking for Grandfather. Mother grabs a scary black pillow, shouts, waves it about, chases the Sirin bird . . . gets rid of it.

Petya tells Tamila about the bird: maybe she knows a spell,
a word to ward off the Sirin bird? But Tamila shakes her head
sadly: no; she used to, but it's back on the glass mountain. She
would give Grandfather her protective toad ring—but then
she'd turn into black powder herself. . . . And she drinks
from her black bottle.

She's so strange! He wanted to think about her, about what
she said, to listen to her dreams; he wanted to sit on her
veranda steps, steps of the house where everything was
allowed: eat bread and jam with unwashed hands, slouch, bite
your nails, walk with your shoes on—if you felt like it—right
in the flowerbeds; and no one shouted, lectured, called for
order, cleanliness, and common sense. You could take a pair of
scissors and cut out a picture you liked from any book—
Tamila didn't care, she was capable of tearing out a picture and
cutting it herself, except she always did it crooked. You could
say whatever came into your head without fear of being
laughed at: Tamila shook her head sadly, understanding; and
if she did laugh, it was as if she were crying. If you ask, she'll
play cards: Go Fish, anything; but she played badly, mixing
up cards and losing.

Everything rational, boring, customary; all that remained
on the other side of the fence overgrown with flowering
bushes.

Ah, he didn't want to leave! At home he had to be quiet
about Tamila (when I grow up and marry her, *then* you'll find
out); and about the Sirin; and about the sparkling egg of the
Alkonost bird, whose owner will be depressed for life. . . .

Petya remembered the egg, got it out of the matchbox,
stuck it under his pillow, and sailed off on *The Flying
Dutchman* over the black nocturnal seas.

In the morning Uncle Borya, with a puffy face, was
smoking before breakfast on the porch. His black beard stuck

out challengingly and his eyes were narrowed in disdain. Seeing his nephew, he began whistling yesterday's disgusting tune . . . and laughed. His teeth—rarely visible because of the beard—were like a wolf's. His black eyebrows crawled upward.

"Greetings to the young romantic." He nodded briskly. "Come on, Peter, saddle up your bike and go to the store. Your mother needs bread, and you can get me two packs of Kazbeks. They'll sell it to you, they will. I know Nina in the store, she'll give kids under sixteen anything at all."

Uncle Borya opened his mouth and laughed. Petya took the ruble and walked his sweaty bike out of the shed. On the ruble, written in tiny letters, were incomprehensible words, left over from Atlantis: *Bir sum. Bir som. Bir manat.* And beneath that, a warning: "Forging state treasury bills is punishable by law." Boring, adult words. The sober morning had swept away the magical evening birds, the girl-fish had gone down to the bottom of the lake, and the golden three-eyed statues of Atlantis slept under a layer of yellow sand. Uncle Borya had dissipated the fragile secrets with his loud, offensive laughter, had thrown out the fairy-tale rubbish—but not forever, Uncle Borya, just for a while. The sun would start leaning toward the west, the air would turn yellow, the oblique rays would spread, and the mysterious world would awaken, start moving, the mute silvery drowned girl would splash her tail, and the heavy, gray Sirin bird would bustle in the fir forest, and in some unpopulated spot, the morning bird Alkonost perhaps already would have hidden its fiery pink egg in a water lily, so that someone could long for things that did not come to pass. . . . *Bir sum, bir som, bir manat.*

Fat-nosed Nina gave him the cigarettes without a word, and asked him to say hello to Uncle Borya—a disgusting hello for a disgusting person—and Petya rode back, ringing his bell, bouncing on the knotty roots that resembled Grandfather's enormous hands. He carefully rode around a dead crow—a wheel had run over the bird, its eye was covered with a white film, the black dragged wings were covered with ashes, and the beak was frozen in a bitter avian smile.

At breakfast Mother looked concerned—Grandfather wouldn't eat again. Uncle Borya whistled, breaking the shell of his egg with a spoon, and watching the boys—looking for something to pick on. Lenechka spilled the milk and Uncle Borya was glad—an excuse to nag. But Lenechka was totally indifferent to his uncle's lectures: he was still little and his soul was sealed like a chicken egg; everything just rolled off. If, God forbid, he fell into the water, he wouldn't drown—he'd turn into a fish, a big-browed striped perch. Lenechka finished his milk and, without listening to the end of the lecture, ran out to the sand box: the sand had dried in the morning sun and his towers must have fallen apart. Petya remembered.

"Mama, did that girl drown a long time ago?"

"What girl?" his mother asked with a start.

"You know. The daughter of that old lady who always asks what time it is?"

"She never had any daughter. What nonsense. She has two grown sons. Who told you that?"

Petya said nothing. Mother looked at Uncle Borya, who laughed with glee.

"Drunken delirium of our shaggy friend! Eh? A girl, eh?"

"What friend?"

"Oh, nothing . . . Neither fish nor fowl."

Petya went out on the porch. Uncle Borya wanted to dirty everything. He wanted to grill the silver girl-fish and crunch her up with his wolf teeth. It won't work, Uncle Borya. The egg of the transparent morning bird Alkonost is glowing under my pillow.

Uncle Borya flung open the window and shouted into the dewy garden: "You should drink less!"

Petya stood by the gate and dug his nail into the ancient gray wood. The day was just beginning.

Grandfather wouldn't eat in the evening, either. Petya sat on the edge of the crumpled bed and patted his grandfather's wrinkled hand. His grandfather was looking out the window, his head turned. The wind had risen, the treetops were swaying, and Mama took down the laundry—it was flapping like *The Flying Dutchman*'s white sails. Glass jangled. The dark garden rose and fell like the ocean. The wind chased the Sirin bird from the branches; flapping its mildewed wings, it flew to the house and sniffed around, moving its triangular face with shut eyes: is there a crack? Mama sent Petya away and made her bed in Grandfather's room.

There was a storm that night. The trees rioted. Lenechka woke up and cried. Morning was gray, sorrowful, windy. The rain knocked Sirin to the ground, and Grandfather sat up in bed and was fed broth. Petya hovered in the doorway, glad to see his grandfather, and looked out the window—the flowers drooped under the rain, and it smelled of autumn. They lit the stove; wearing hooded jackets, they carried wood from the shed. There was nothing to do outside. Lenechka sat down to draw, Uncle Borya paced, hands behind his back, and whistled.

The day was boring: they waited for lunch and then waited for dinner. Grandfather ate a hard-boiled egg. It rained again at night.

That night Petya wandered around underground passages, staircases, in subway tunnels; he couldn't find the exit, kept changing trains: the trains traveled on ladders with the doors wide open and they passed through strange rooms filled with furniture; Petya had to get out, get outside, get up to where

Lenechka and Grandfather were in danger: they forgot to shut
the door, it was wide open, and the Sirin bird was walking up
the creaking steps, its eyes shut; Petya's schoolbag was in the
way, but he needed it. How to get out? Where was the exit?
How do I get upstairs? "You need a bill." Of course, a bill to
get out. There was the booth. Give me a bill. A treasury bill?
Yes, yes, please! "Forging state treasury bills is punishable by
law." There they were, the bills: long, black sheets of paper.
Wait, they have holes in them. That's punishable by law. Give
me some more. I don't want to! The schoolbag opens, and long
black bills, holes all over, fall out. Hurry, pick them up,
quick, I'm being persecuted, they'll catch me. They scatter all
over the floor, Petya picks them up, stuffing them in any
which way; the crowd separates, someone is being led
through. . . . He can't get out of the way, so many bills, oh
there it is, the horrible thing: they're leading it by the arms,
huge, howling like a siren, its purple gaping face upraised; it's
neither-fish-nor-fowl, it's the end!

Petya jumped up with a pounding heart; it wasn't light yet.
Lenechka slept peacefully. He crept barefoot to Grandfather's
room, pushed the door—silence. The night light was on. The
black oxygen pillows were in the corner. Grandfather lay with
open eyes, hands clutching the blanket. He went over, feeling
cold; guessing, he touched Grandfather's hand and recoiled.
Mama!

No, Mama will scream and be scared. Maybe it can still be
fixed. Maybe Tamila can help?

Petya rushed to the exit—the door was wide open. He stuck
his bare feet into rubber boots, put a hood over his head, and
rattled down the steps. The rain had ended, but it still dripped
from the trees. The sky was turning gray. He ran on legs that
buckled and slipped in the mud. He pushed the veranda door.
There was a strong waft of cold, stale smoke. Petya bumped

into a small table: a jangle and rolling sound. He bent down, felt around, and froze: the ring with the toad, Tamila's protection, was on the floor. There was noise in the bedroom. Petya flung open the door. There were two silhouettes in the dim light in the bed: Tamila's tangled black hair on the pillow, her black robe on the chair; she turned and moaned. Uncle Borya sat up in bed, his beard up, his hair disheveled. Tossing the blanket over Tamila's leg and covering his own legs, he blustered and shouted, peering into the dark: "Eh? Who is it? What is it? Eh!"

Petya started crying and shouted, trembling in horrible understanding, "Grandfather's dead! Grandfather's dead! Grandfather's dead!"

Uncle Borya threw back the blanket and spat out horrible, snaking, inhuman words; Petya shuddered in sobs, and ran out blindly: boots in the flowerbeds; his soul was boiled like egg white hanging in clumps on the trees rushing toward him; sour sorrow filled his mouth and he reached the lake and fell down under the wet tree oozing rain; screeching, kicking his feet, he chased Uncle Borya's horrible words, Uncle Borya's horrible legs, from his mind.

He got used to it, quieted down, lay there. Drops fell on him from above. The dead lake, the dead forest: birds fell from the trees and lay feet up; the dead empty world was filled with gray thick oozing depression. Everything was a lie.

He felt something hard in his hand and unclenched his fist. The squashed silver guard toad popped its eyes at him.

The match box, radiating eternal longing, lay in his pocket.

The Sirin bird had suffocated Grandfather.

No one can escape his fate. It's all true, child. That's how it is.

He lay there a bit longer, wiped his face, and headed for the house.

SWEET
DREAMS,
SON

In 1948 Sergei's mother-in-law's karakul fur coat was swiped.

The fur coat, of course, was marvelous—curly, warm, with a rare lining: lilies of the valley embroidered in purple. You could stay in a coat like that forever: shoes on your feet, a muff on your hands, and just go, go, go! And the way they swiped it—brazenly, boorishly, crudely—just snatched it out from under her nose! His mother-in-law—a gorgeous creature, plucked eyebrows, heels clicking—went off to the flea market taking the cleaning woman Panya with her—you don't remember her, Lenochka. No, Lenochka did remember her vaguely. Don't be silly, weren't you born in 1950? You're confusing her with Klava, remember Klava, she had that pink comb and she was so round, remember? She kept saying, "My sins are great, my sins are great," and kept worrying she'd burn in hell. But what a cook, and she taught me. And we used to give her our old shoes for her grandchildren in the village. Now no one takes old shoes, you don't know what to do with them.

So anyway, she went with Panya. That Panya . . . His mother-in-law wanted to buy another fur coat, squirrel fur, for every day. A lady was selling one—a decent-looking woman, teary-eyed, with a blue nose; I can see her now . . . She had Panya hold the karakul, she put on the squirrel, turned around—the lady's trail was cold and the karakul was gone. Panya, where's the coat? A shriek, tears: Madame, I don't know what happened, I was just holding it a second ago. They distracted my eyes, damn them! Well, who knows about her eyes, but couldn't it have been a conspiracy? It was after the war, times were rough, there were all sorts of gangs around, and who really knew that Panya? And naturally the envy, the profound disapproval of people like his mother-in-law, Maria Maximovna, pretty, flashy, dressed warm and rich. And for what reason? You'd think they were living like birds of paradise, she and Pavel Antonovich, but nothing of the sort. Constant tension, anxiety, separations, night work. Pavel Antonovich was a military doctor, a warrior against the plague, an elderly man, complex, quick to judge; terrible in his wrath, and honest in his work. Here was an opportunity to look at a photograph of Pavel Antonovich, the way he was in the last years of his life, insulted, abandoned, wounded by the classic situation: his students moved on, taking the most precious of their teacher's work, carrying the slightly soiled banner onward without honoring the founder with a single line or a single footnote.

Sergei raised his eyes on high and made out, high on the

wall, in the warm silky shadows, a pair of glasses, a
mustache. . . . Lenochka, do you remember Papa? Of course.
Maria Maximovna went to the kitchen to get sweet rolls,
Sergei leaned over to pat Lenochka's hand; she offered it to him
as if it were an object and explained that actually she barely
remembered her father and had only said that for Mother's
sake. . . . She remembered the settled March snow, full of
holes, the lacquered shine of the car, and how it smelled
inside, and the chauffeur's steel teeth, his cap . . . The cloud
of her father's cologne, the creak of the seat, his angry nape,
and the naked trees flashing past the window—they were
going somewhere . . . And another day—May, golden, with
a harsh sweet wind coming through the window, and the
apartment upside down, either the carpets being sent to the
cleaners or the winter things being put away in mothballs,
everything shifted, people running back and forth. And Pavel
Antonovich's wrathful horrible shout in the hallway, thumping footsteps on the floor; he throws something heavy, bursts
into the room, and powerful and red, he pushes through,
trampling the teddy bear, trampling the doll's tea, and the
May sun was indignant, shaking and splashing from the lenses
of his glasses. The reason was trifling—the dog might have
made a mess near the door. But in fact the dog was nothing,
an excuse, it was just that life had begun to turn its not-good
side toward Pavel Antonovich. And they didn't have anything
to drive in, anymore.

His mother-in-law returned with the rolls and fresh tea,
Lenochka put her hand back in its place, a used object.
Lenochka was rather cool for a new bride, she smiled too
politely, she burned at half-steam; and what was hidden, what
thoughts flashed behind those watercolor eyes? Pale cheeks,
hair like seaweed along those cheeks, weak hands, light
feet—it was all enchanting, and even though Sergei basically

liked his women sturdy, colorful, and black-browed, like the
dolls made in Vyatka, he could not resist Lenochka's watery
charms. She entwined herself around him, not hot, her soul
friable and inaccessible, with puny female problems: a cough;
my shoes are too big; drive a nail in right there, Seryozha—he
hammered, twisting the shoes as small as saucers in his hands,
everything falls off the tiny Snow Fairy—and rubbed Lenochka's narrow back with oil of turpentine.

He married in fear and delight, hazarding a guess, understanding nothing: neither who Lenochka was nor why he had
chosen her; he'd find out with time. She was a frail girl, and
he was her protector and support, and his mother-in-law was
a sweet lady, amiable and tolerably silly, a home economics
teacher. She taught girls to sew aprons, to bind seams, or
something. Theory of sewing, the basics of fire safety. "A
stitch is the intertwining of thread with fabric between two
needle punctures." "A fire is the burning of objects not
intended for burning." Cozy, feminine work. At home, there
was family coziness, the family hearth, the modest and
respectable space of a three-room apartment, the legacy of the
severe Pavel Antonovich. The hallway was lined with books,
something was always cooking in the kitchen, and beyond the
kitchen was a tiny room, a cell—they always built this way,
Seryozha dear, for the maids; this is where that horrible Panya
lived, and Klava with the pink comb: do you want me to turn
it into your study, a man needs a study of his own. Of course
he liked. A small room, but totally his now—what could be
better? The table by the window, the chair here, a bookshelf
behind him. In the summer, poplar fluff would fly in through
the window, and birdsong and children's voices . . . Your
hand, Maria Maximovna. Allow me to kiss it. There, isn't
everything fine?

Why, she can't even imagine how fine it is, what a miracle,

what a gift from the gods that room and that family were—for him, an orphan, a boy without a name, without a father, a mother. They invented it all for him at the orphanage: name, surname, age. He had no childhood, his childhood had been burnt up, bombed at an unknown railroad station; someone pulled him out of the fire, threw him on the ground, turning him over and over, slapping his head with a fur hat to put out the flames. . . . He hadn't understood that the hat had saved him, a big black smelly hat—it knocked the memory out of him, he had nightmares about that hat, it screamed and blew up and deafened him—he had stammered a long time afterward, crying and covering his head with his hands when they tried to dress him at the home. How old had he been—three, four? And now, in the mid-70s, he, a grown man, felt his heart flipflop when he passed a store with fur hats on display. He would stop and stare, forcing himself to do it, trying to remember: Who am I? Where am I from? Whose son am I? After all, I did have a mother, someone gave birth to me, loved me, was taking me somewhere.

In the summer he played on trampled playgrounds with children just like him, burned and nameless, pulled out from under wheels. They held hands and formed two lines. "Ali Baba, hey!" "What do you say?" "Pull the line away!" "From which end of the day?" "From dawn and send Seryozha this way." And he would run in his gray orphanage pants from one line to the other, from his family into another, to push apart the thin clasped hands, and to join them, the strangers, if he could, feeling proud of his strength yet a little treacherous too.

Long winters, hungry eyes, shaved heads, some adult giving a quick pat on the head as he ran past; the smell of mice in the sheets, the dull light. The older boys beat him, demanded that he steal for them, tempting him with a chunk of undercooked bread under his nose—we'll share it with you, climb through that narrow window, you're skinny, you'll squeeze through. But someone invisible and inaudible seemed to be shaking her head, eyes closed: *don't, don't take it.* Was it his mother, giving him a sign from dark, shattered time, from the other side, beyond the hat; were incorporeal powers protecting him? He finished school and his file said: "Morally stable, orderly." His longing for his mother, who was nowhere, ate away at him quietly. The idea that in the final analysis, everyone was descended from the apes, somehow did not console him. He invented mothers for himself, imagined himself the son of a favorite teacher—she had lost a small boy and she was looking for him, asking everyone if they had seen him. Skinny and afraid of a hat? And he, he was right there, in the front row, and she didn't even know it. She would take a good look and cry out, "Seryozha, is that you? Why didn't you say anything?" He was the son of the cook—he helped slice bread in the kitchen, glancing at her white cap and quick hands, trembling, waiting for the recognition to come; he stared at women in the street—in vain, they all ran past.

Now, keeping it secret from Lenochka, he wanted to be the son of Maria Maximovna. Hadn't she had a son who burned to death in some distant, nameless railroad station? The burning of objects not intended for burning? . . . The cozy room beyond the kitchen, snow beyond the window, the yellow lamp shade, the old wallpaper with maple leaves, the old house—if he could only remember. . . Didn't it seem as if he had lived here, as if he were recognizing something? . . .

Nonsense; Maria Maximovna never had a lost boy, the only thing she lost was the fur coat, a good fur coat with a silk lining embroidered with purple lilies of the valley. Pavel Antonovich, a big man with a lot of stars on his uniform, took that luxurious item from a hook on a wall in a German house—he liked it and he didn't waste time. He took it and sent it back home.

What a fur coat it had been. What a shame, Seryozha. You must know the vile feeling of being robbed. I didn't even have time to turn around, even to gasp—they switched them. Stuck me with the cheap squirrel coat, and not even new, as I learned later: it fell apart at the seams. I think it must have been stolen. Just imagine the situation—Pavel Antonovich's wife robbed, and wearing a stolen coat. . . The worst part was having to confess that I had gone to the flea market: I had done it on the sly. . . . Oh, it was terrible just to look at him: a geyser of anger. Robbed . . . He couldn't stand things like that. He, a military doctor, an honored man who had given his whole life to science—and to people—and then something like this. People were in great awe of him then, it was later that they calumnied him, insulted him, forced him into retirement—him, such a respected specialist in infectious diseases. They forgot all his achievements, his bravery and courage, forgot how he had battled the plague in the twenties and thirties—and how he conquered it, Seryozha. Risking his life every minute. He had no patience for cowards.

It's a horrible thing, the plague. You don't hear too much about it nowadays, just the rare case here or there—which, incidentally, is thanks to Pavel Antonovich—but back then it was an epidemic. Infected steppes, villages, whole regions . . . Pavel Antonovich and his colleagues set up experiments: who is spreading the plague? All right, rats; but which kind? Just imagine; it turned out that all kinds of rats were responsible. Domestic, attic, ship, sewer, migrant rats. Moreover, all those innocent-looking bunnies, gophers, even little mice . . . Gerbils, hamsters, moles. Look, I couldn't believe my ears when Pavel Antonovich told me, but he insisted: camels. Understand? You can't trust anyone. Who would have thought? Yes, yes, camels get the plague too. And can you imagine what it's like doing experiments on camels? Camels are huge. They had to catch one, infect it, take samples from it; and all by themselves, with their own hands. They kept it penned up, fed it, shoveled its manure. And it didn't want to give samples, and it spat at them, too—plague-ridden spit. And it tried to hit them in the face.

I tell you, doctors are saints, I always say that. And then . . . ? And then, when they are sure an animal is infected, they put it to sleep, of course. What else could they do? It would infect the others, wouldn't it?

Then the war began and Pavel Antonovich was reassigned. Yes, it meant even more work. The war, the war . . . Why am I telling you about it, you went through all that yourself?

It was during the war that they met, his mother-in-law and Pavel Antonovich. They married and saw each other sporadically. He liked that she was so young and lively . . . He wanted to dress her nicely, that's why he sent the fur. . . . And he was pleased with it too: why don't you wear the fur, Mashenka. . . . He worried about it, got mothballs for the summer. And then a blow like that . . .

A gentle, marvelous, understanding woman, that Maria Maximovna. Just one quirk—can't forget that fur coat. She's a woman, those things are important to them. We all have our own memories. She tells him about her fur coat, Sergei tells her about the fur hat. She sympathized. Lenochka smiled at both, soaring in her vague thoughts. Lenochka is steady and passionless, a sister instead of a wife. Mother and sister—what more could a lost boy want?

Sergei put up shelves in his cubbyhole and placed favorite books on them. If only he could put a cot in there, too. But he went to sleep in the bedroom with Lenochka. At night he lay sleepless, looking at her quiet face with pink shadows near the eyes, and wondered: who is she? What does she think about, what does she dream? If you ask, she shrugs and says nothing. Never raises her voice, if he tracks snow into the house she doesn't notice, if he smokes in the bedroom she doesn't care. . . . She reads whatever comes her way. If it's Camus, fine; if it's Sergeyev-Tsensky, that's fine, too. She gave off a chill. The daughter of mustachioed, bespectacled Pavel Antonovich . . . Strange.

Pavel Antonovich . . . He hangs on the wall in the living room, in a frame, and night shadows cross his face. An oak grew and collapsed. Collapsed a long time ago, Lenochka doesn't even remember him. But he's still here—wandering up and down the hallway, making the floorboards creak, touching the doorknob. He runs his finger along the wallpaper, the maple leaves, along the bookshelves—he left his daughter a good inheritance. Listens for the squeak of a rat. Domestic, attic, field, ship, migrant . . . You animal, you, tell me your name: are you the death of me? will you eat me? I'm not your death, I won't eat you: I'm just a bunny, a gray bunny. . . . Rabbits also carry plague. A particularly dangerous infection . . . The prognosis is extremely poor. . . . In case of suspected infection with the plague send an urgent report. . . . The patients and everyone who has been in contact with them will be quarantined. Was he afraid? Such an important man. Terrible in his wrath and honest in his work. But why that fur coat?

And what if Pavel Antonovich were Sergei's father? What if he had had another wife before Maria Maximovna? Surface out of nonexistence, take on a sturdy chain of ancestors—Pavel Antonovich, Anton Felixovich, Felix Kazimirovich . . . Why not? It's a realistic possibility. . . .

He took the fur coat from the hook, turned it inside out—fur inside, lilies of the valley outside—and the tissue paper rustled. Twine! *Bitte.* He rested his knee on the package, pulled tight, knotted the twine with his clean medical fingers. One more knot. Tugged—it'll hold. He took it, he stooped to that. For the tangled tracks, the explosion, his son's singed head, the mother who went up in flames, the hat that knocked out the child's memory. The face with the closed eyes floated up again, shaking its head: *don't,* don't take it. Father, don't take it! Three years later, it was stolen at the market. How he shouted! Panya, the maid, was in on it, naturally. Think about it—to disappear like that, in the twinkling of an eye. . . . Naturally, it was a gang. Maria Maximovna would have let it go, but Pavel Antonovich, with his character, simply could not bear it. Panya had to be arrested. Yes, yes! To whom did you pass the fur coat? Who are your co-conspirators? When did you enter into a criminal conspiracy? How much were you supposed to get for fingering the job? Panya was a stupid woman, uneducated, and she babbled some nonsense, gave conflicting testimony; it was disgusting to hear. In short— they convicted her. But the coat was never found. Gone. Warm, curly, with the silky, slippery lining.

"I'm hearing this for the fifth time," Sergei said, angrily pulling the blanket over himself.

"So what? Mother is still upset."

"Yes, but how long can she keep it up? You'd think she's a suffering Akaky Akakiyevich without his overcoat!"

"I don't understand you. What is it, are your sympathies with the thieves?"

"What does that have to do with it. . . . And besides, didn't he steal it?"

"Papa? Papa was the most honest of men."

An uneducated woman, that Panya. She split, vanished, disappeared. A village woman, her husband died at the front. The pink comb. No, Klava had the comb. No face, no voice—just a total blank. He was Panya's son. Perhaps; perhaps. His father died, and she fled with him through swamps, sinking; pushed her way through forests, tripping;

begged for hot water at railroad stations, wailing. The train, the explosion. The tracks turned into corkscrews, the hat across his face, the black hat to knock out his memory. You lie there, peering into the dark—deeper, deeper, to the limit—no, there's a wall there. Panya lost him at the station. She was taken away unconscious. She woke up—where's Seryozha? Or Petya, Vitya, Yegorushka? Someone must have seen them putting out a burning boy. She goes, seeking him from town to town. Opens all the doors, knocks at all the windows: have you seen him? A dark kerchief and sunken eyes . . . Takes a job working for Pavel Antonovich. Are you the death of me, will you eat me? No, I'm a bunny, a gray bunny. "Panya, come with me, you'll hold my fur coat." Wait, don't go! "Mistress, I've lost my son, what do I care for your coat?" Let her stay home. And another twenty-five years in that room. Then Sergei marries Lenochka, comes to the house, Panya takes a good look and recognizes him. . . . She couldn't have stolen it, she had shut her eyes and shook her head: don't take it. In case of suspected incident send an urgent report. Domestic, attic, migrant, field . . . Silk lining. Seryozha, drive a nail there.

All right, what if she *did* steal it! Impoverished, starving like those thieving boys, her house burned down, her son lost, her husband dead in the swamps. What if she had been tempted by the purple lilies of the valley? I won't hammer a nail into her. I am her son. Panya is my mother, that's decided, everyone must know. Why did he take the coat from the hook? That coat belonged to Panya's husband, he should have reached it, crawled there, extended his scorched hand toward it—no, he wouldn't have taken it, he wouldn't have stooped to that. But you, high and mighty gentleman, you stooped. And I am married to your daughter. Pavel Antonovich is my father. Otherwise why does he torment me with the

lost fur coat, rustling his medals, sighing behind the wall?
Tell me your name. Holding hands tightly, the chain of
ancestors walks into the depths, sinking into the dark jelly of
time. Stand with us, nameless one, join us. Find your link in
the chain. Pavel Antonovich, Anton Felixovich, Felix Kazimirovich. You are our descendant, you lay on our bed, loved
Lenochka without blinking an eye, you ate our sweet rolls—
every single currant in them we had to tear away from
domestic, attic, and field rats; for you we coughed up horrible
phlegm and let our nodes swell, for you we infected camels
that spat in our face—you can't get away from us. We built
this for you, you nameless and clean boy, this house, this
hearth, kitchen, hallway, bedroom, cubby, we lit the lamps
and set up the books. We punished those who lifted their
hands to steal our property. Ali Baba, hey! What do you say?
Pull the line away. From which end of the day?

Panya stole from family. But Pavel Antonovich stole from
strangers. Panya confessed. Pavel Antonovich suffered from
slander. The scales of justice are balanced. And what did you
do? You came, you ate, you judged? In anti-plague goggles
and rubber boots, with an enormous syringe, Pavel Antonovich approached the camel. I am your death, I'll eat you up!
Mice get sick, and so do rabbits. Everyone gets sick. Everyone.
No need to brag.

Lenochka did not wish to hear about Sergei's hat anymore.
As if there were nothing else to talk about. And really . . .
Children, don't shout! I don't understand who she is. Why she
married me. If she doesn't care about anything . . . She's
waterlogged. . . . Not a person, but soap suds. Seryozha,
you're shouting so loudly. Just like Pavel Antonovich. Hush,
hush. In her condition, Lenochka needs peace.

Lenochka, don't be mad at me. All right, all right,
Seryozha. Drive a nail there—to hang up the diapers. Why

don't you sleep in the study, won't little Antosha let you get any sleep? The shadow of leaves falls on the tiny face, the lace-trimmed sheet; the infant sleeps, his wrinkled fists raised, his brow furrowed—struggling to understand something. The fishies are asleep in the pond. The birdies are asleep in the trees. Who's breathing outside in the garden? We don't care, my love.

Sweet dreams, sonny, you're not to blame for anything at all. The plague corpses in the cemetery are covered with lime, the poppies on the steppe bring sweet dreams, the camels are locked up in the zoos, warm leaves rustle and whisper over your head. What about? What do you care?

SONYA

A person lived—a person died. Only the name remains—Sonya. "Remember, Sonya used to say . . ." "A dress like Sonya's . . ." "You keep blowing your nose all the time, like Sonya . . ." Then even the people who used to say that died, and there was only a trace of her voice in my head, incorporeal, seeming to come from the black jaws of the telephone receiver. Or all of a sudden there is a view of a sunny room, like a bright photograph come to life—laughter around a set table, like those hyacinths in a glass vase on the tablecloth, wreathed too with curly pink smiles. Look quickly, before it goes out. Who is that? Is the one you need among them? But the bright room trembles and fades and now the backs of the seated people are translucent

like gauze, and with frightening speed, their laughter falls to
pieces, recedes in the distance—catch it if you can.

No, wait, let me look at you. Sit as you were and call out
your names in order. But it is futile to try grasping recollec-
tions with clumsy corporeal hands. The merry laughing figure
turns into a large, crudely painted rag doll and will fall off its
chair if it's not propped up; on its meaningless forehead are
drips of glue from the moplike wig; the blue glassy eyes are
joined inside the empty skull by a metal arc with a lead ball for
counterweight. Just look at that, the old hag! When you think
she pretended to be alive and loved. But the laughing company
has flown up and away, and contrary to the iron laws of space
and time is chattering away in some inaccessible corner of
the world, incorruptible unto eternity, festively immortal, and
might even appear again at some turn in the road—at the most
inappropriate moment, and of course without warning.

Well, if that's the way you are, so be it. Chasing you is like
catching butterflies waving a shovel. But I would like to learn
more about Sonya.

One thing is clear—Sonya was an utter fool. No one has
ever disputed that quality of hers, and now there is no one to
do it anyway. Invited out to dinner for the first time, in the
distant, yellowish-smoke-shrouded year of 1930, she sat like a
dummy at the end of a long, starched table, in front of a
napkin cone folded into a house, as was then customary. The
bouillon pond cooled. The idle spoon lay before her. The
dignity of all the kings of England froze Sonya's equine
features.

"And you, Sonya," they said to her (they must have
addressed her more formally, using her patronymic, hopelessly
lost now), "and you, Sonya, why aren't you eating?"

"Waiting for the pepper," she replied severely with her icy
upper lip.

Actually, after some time had passed and Sonya's irreplaceability in the kitchen for pre-party preparations and her sewing skills and her willingness to take other people's children for walks and even babysit if the whole noisy group was heading for some unpostponable festivity became evident—with the passage of time, the crystal of Sonya's stupidity sparkled with other facets, exquisite in its unpredictability. A sensitive instrument, Sonya's soul apparently captured the tonality of the mood of the society that had sheltered her yesterday, but, gawking, she failed to attune herself to today's mood. So, if Sonya gaily shouted out, "Bottoms up!" at a wake, it was clear she was still at somebody's birthday party; while at weddings, Sonya's toasts gave off the gloom of yesterday's funeral meats.

"I saw you yesterday at the concert with a beautiful lady; I wonder, who was she?" Sonya would ask a bewildered husband as she leaned across his stiffened wife. At moments like that, the mocker Lev Adolfovich would purse his lips, arch his eyebrows, and shake his head, his shallow glasses glinting. "If a person is dead, that's for a long time; if he's stupid, that's forever." Well, that's just what happened, time merely confirmed his words.

Lev Adolfovich's sister, Ada, a sharp, thin woman of serpentine elegance who was once discomfited by Sonya's idiocy, dreamed of punishing her. Just a little, of course, so they could have a laugh and give the little fool some amusement. And they whispered in a corner—Lev and Ada— plotting something witty.

So, Sonya sewed. . . . And how did she dress? Most unbecomingly, friends, most unbecomingly. Something blue, striped, so unflattering. Just imagine: a head like a Przewalski's horse (Lev Adolfovich noted that), under her jaw the huge dangling bow of her blouse sticking out from her suit's stiff lapels, and the sleeves were always too long. Sunken chest, legs so fat they looked as if they came from a different person's set, enormous feet. She wore down her shoes on one side. Well, her chest and legs, that's not clothing. . . . Yes it is, my dear, it counts as clothing too. You have to take features like that into account, some things you just can't wear at all. . . . She had a brooch, an enamel dove. She wore it on the lapel of her jacket, never parted with it. And when she changed into another dress, she always pinned on that dove.

Sonya was a good cook. She whipped up marvelous cakes. And then that, you know, offal, innards—kidneys, udders, brains—it's so easy to ruin them, but she made them wonderfully. So those dishes were always assigned to her. It was delicious and an excuse for jokes. Lev Adolfovich, pursing his lips, would call across the table: "Sonechka, your udders simply astonish me today!" And she would nod happily in reply. And Ada would say in a sweet voice, "I, for one, am enraptured by your sheep's brains." "They're veal," Sonya would reply, not understanding, smiling. And everyone enjoyed it; wasn't it just too much?

She liked children, that was clear, and you could go on vacation, even to Kislovodsk, and leave the children and the apartment in her care—why don't you live at our place for a while, Sonya, all right?—and find everything in perfect order upon your return: the furniture dusted, the children rosy-cheeked and fed, and they played outside every day and even went on field trips to the museum where Sonya worked as some sort of curator; those museum curators lead a boring life, they're all old maids. The children would become attached to her and be sad when she had to be transferred to another family. But you can't be egoists and hog Sonya; others might need her, too. In general, they managed, setting up a sensible queuing system.

Well, what else can I say about her? Basically, I think that's it. Who remembers any details now? Fifty years later there's almost no one left alive. And there were so many truly interesting, really worthwhile people, who left behind concert recordings, books, monographs on art. What fates! You could talk endlessly about any of them. Take Lev Adolfovich, a bastard basically, but a brilliant man and in some ways a pussycat. You could ask Ada Adolfovna, but she's pushing ninety, I think, and . . . you understand . . . Something happened to her during the siege of Leningrad. Related to Sonya, incidentally. No, I don't remember it very well. Something about a glass, and some letters, a joke of some sort.

How old was Sonya? In 1941—when her tracks break off—she should have been forty. Yes, I think that's it. From that it's easy to figure out when she was born and so forth, but what difference could that make if we don't know who her parents were, what she was like as a child, where she lived, what she did, and who her friends were up to the day when she came into the world out of nebulousness and sat down to wait for the pepper in the sunny, festive dining room?

Of course, we must believe she was a romantic and, in her own way, lofty. After all, those bows of hers, and the enamel dove, and the poetry quotations, always sentimental, that flew from her lips inappositely, as if spat by her long upper lip that revealed her long ivory-colored teeth, and her love of children—and any children at that—all that characterizes her quite unambiguously. A romantic creature. Was she happy? Oh, yes! That's certain. You can say what you want, but she was happy.

And just think—life is full of such tricks—she owed her happiness completely to Ada Adolfovna, that snake. (Too bad you didn't know her in her youth. An interesting woman.)

A whole group of them got together—Ada, Lev, and Valerian, Seryozha, I think, and Kotik, and someone else—

and worked out this practical joke (since the idea was Ada's, Lev called it "a plan from Ades"), which turned out to be a great success. This must have been around 1933. Ada was in her prime, though no longer a girl—marvelous figure, dusky face with dark rose cheeks, she was number one at tennis, number one at kayaking, everyone thought she was terrific. Ada was even embarrassed by having so many suitors when Sonya had none. (What a joke! Suitors for Sonya?) And she suggested inventing a mysterious admirer for the poor thing, someone madly in love with her but who had reasons why he couldn't meet her personally. Excellent idea. The phantom was created instantly, named Nikolai, burdened with a wife and three children, and moved into Ada's father's apartment for purposes of correspondence—here protests were voiced: what if Sonya learns, what if she sticks her nose in there?—but the argument was rejected as insubstantial. First of all, Sonya was stupid, that was the point; and secondly, she had a conscience—Nikolai had a family, she wouldn't try to break it up. There, he wrote quite clearly, Nikolai did: darling, your unforgettable visage is imprinted forever on my wounded heart ("Don't write 'wounded,' she'll take it literally that he's an invalid!"), but we are fated never, ever to be near because of my duty to my children . . . and so on. But my feeling, Nikolai continues—no, sincere feeling is better—will warm my cold members ("What do you mean, Adochka!" "Don't bother me, you idiots!") a pathfinding star and all that other *moon-june-spoon.* A letter like that. Let's say he saw her at a concert, admired her fine profile (here Valerian fell off the couch laughing), and now wants to start up a lofty correspondence. He found out her address with difficulty. Begs for a photograph. Why can't he meet for a date, the children won't be in the way for that? He has a sense of duty. But for some reason they don't keep him from writing, do they? Well, then he's paralyzed. From the waist down. Hence the chilled members. Listen, stop fooling around. If necessary, we'll paralyze him later. Ada sprinkled Chypre cologne on the stationery, Kotik pulled a dried forget-me-not from his childhood herbarium, pink with age, and stuck it in the envelope. Life was fun!

The correspondence was stormy on both sides. Sonya, the fool, went for it right away. She fell in love so hard you couldn't drag her away. They had to rein in her ardor: Nikolai wrote about one letter a month, braking Sonya and her raging cupid. Nikolai expressed himself in poetry: Valerian had to sweat a bit. There were pearls there, if you understood— Nikolai compared Sonya to a lily, a liana, and a gazelle, and himself simultaneously to a nightingale and an antelope. Ada wrote the prose text and served as general director, stopping her silly friends and their suggestions to Valerian: "Write that she's a gnu. In the sense of an antelope. My divine gnu, I perish anew without you."

Ada was in top form: she quivered with Nikolai's tenderness and revealed the depths of his lonely, stormy spirit, insisted on the necessity of preserving the platonic purity of their relations, and at the same time hinted at the destructive passion, whose time to be displayed for some reason had not yet come. Of course, in the evenings, Nikolai and Sonya had to lift their eyes to the same star at an appointed hour. Couldn't do without that. If the participants in the epistolary novel were nearby at the appointed minute, they tried to keep Sonya from parting the curtains and sneaking a glance at the starry heights, calling her into the hallway: "Sonya, come here a moment. Sonya, here's what—" relishing her confusion: the significant instant was approaching, and Nikolai's gaze was in danger of hanging around in vain in the neighborhood of Sirius or whatever it was called—you generally had to look in the direction of Pulkovo Observatory.

Then the joke got boring: how long could they go on, especially since they could get absolutely nothing out of languid Sonya, no secrets; she didn't want any bosom buddies and pretended nothing was going on. Just think how secretive she turned out to be, while she burned with unquenchable flames of high feeling in her letters, promising Nikolai eternal fidelity and telling him about every little thing: what she dreamed and what she had heard little birds twittering. She sent wagon loads of dried flowers in envelopes, and for one of Nikolai's birthdays she sent him her only ornament, taking it off her ugly jacket: the white enamel dove. "Sonya, where's your dove?" "It flew off," she said, revealing her ivory equine teeth, and you couldn't read anything in her eyes. Ada kept planning to kill off Nikolai, who was turning into a pain, but when she got the dove she shuddered and put the murder off for a better time. In the letter that came with the dove, Sonya swore to give her life for Nikolai or follow him, if necessary, to the ends of the earth.

The whole imaginable crop of laughter had been harvested, damned Nikolai was like a ball and chain underfoot, but it would have been inhumane to abandon Sonya alone on the road without her dove, without her love. The years passed: Valerian, Kotik, and, I think, Seryozha dropped out of the game for various reasons, and Ada carried the epistolary weight alone, hostilely baking monthly hot kisses by mail, like a machine. She had even begun to turn a little like Nikolai herself and at times in evening light she fancied she could see a mustache on her tanned pink face as she looked in the mirror. And so two women in two parts of Leningrad, one in hate, the other in love, wrote letters to each other about a person who had never existed.

When the war began, neither had time to evacuate. Ada dug ditches thinking about her son, taken out of the city with his kindergarten. No time for love. She ate everything she could find, boiled her leather shoes, drank hot bouillon made from wallpaper—that had a little paste, at least. December came, everything ended. Ada took her father on a sled to a common grave; and then Lev Adolfovich; fueled the stove with Dickens and with stiff fingers wrote Sonya Nikolai's farewell letter. She wrote that it was all a lie, that she hated everyone, that Sonya was a stupid old fool and a horse, that none of it had been here and damn you all to hell. Neither Ada nor Nikolai wanted to go on living. She unlocked the doors of her father's big apartment to make it easier for the funeral brigade to get in and lay down on the couch, piling her father's and her brother's coats on top of her.

It's not clear what happened next. First of all, hardly anyone was interested; and secondly, Ada Adolfovna isn't very talkative, besides which, as I've already said, there's time! Time has devoured everything. Let's add that it's hard to read other people's souls: it's dark and not everyone knows how to do it. Vague conclusions, attempts at answers—nothing more.

I doubt Sonya received Nikolai's graveside song. Letters didn't get through that black December, or else took months. Let's suppose that raising her eyes, half-blind with starvation, to the evening star over bombed-out Pulkovo, she did not feel the magnetic gaze of her beloved that day and realized his hour had come. A loving heart—say what you will—feels such things, you can't trick it. And realizing that it was time, ready to turn to ashes in order to save her one and only, Sonya took everything she had—a can of prewar tomato juice, saved for a matter of life and death like this—and made her way across all of Leningrad to the dying Nikolai's apartment. There was exactly enough juice for one life.

Nikolai lay under a mound of coats, in a hat with ear flaps, with a horrible black face, caked lips, but smooth-shaven. Sonya sank to her knees, pressed her eyes to his swollen hand with its broken fingernails, and wept a bit. Then she spoon-fed him some juice, threw a few books onto the fire, blessed her lucky fate, and left with a pail to get some water, never to return. The bombing was heavy that day.

That, basically, is all that can be said about Sonya. A person lived—a person died. Only the name remains.

"Ada Adolfovna, give me Sonya's letters."

Ada Adolfovna rolls from the bedroom to the dining room, turning the big wheels of her chair with her hands. Her wrinkled face twitches. A black dress covers her lifeless legs to her toes. A large cameo is pinned near her throat, someone is killing something on it: shields, spears, the enemy gracefully fallen.

"Letters?"

"Letters, letters, give me Sonya's letters!"

"I can't hear you!"

"She never can hear the word 'give,' " her nephew's wife hisses in irritation, narrowing her eyes at the cameo.

"Isn't it time for dinner?" Ada Adolfovna smacks her lips.

What large dark cupboards, what heavy silverware in them, and vases, and all kinds of supplies: tea, jam, grains, macaroni. In the other rooms there are more cupboards, cupboards, chiffonniers, wardrobes—with linens, books, all kinds of things. Where does she keep the packet of Sonya's letters, an old package wrapped with twine, crackling with dried flowers, yellowed and translucent like dragonfly wings? Does she not remember, or does she not want to tell? And what's the point in pestering a trembling paralyzed old woman? Didn't she have enough hard days in her life? Most probably she threw the packet into the fire, standing on her swollen knees that icy winter, in the blazing circle of a minute's light, and perhaps the letters, starting slowly at first and then quickly blackening at the corners and finally swirling up in a column of roaring flames, warmed her contorted, frozen fingers, if only for a brief instant. Let it be so. But she must have taken the white dove out of there, I think. After all, doves don't burn.

THE
FAKIR

Filin—as usual, unexpectedly—appeared in the telephone receiver with an invitation: to have a look at his new love. The evening's program was clear: a crisp white tablecloth, light, warmth, special puff-pastry *pirozhki* à la Tmutarakan, the nicest music coming from somewhere in the ceiling, and engrossing conversation. Blue curtains everywhere, cupboards with his collections, beads hanging along the walls. Then there might be new toys: a snuffbox with a portrait of a lady in transports over her own pink naked powderiness, a beaded purse, perhaps an Easter egg, or something else useless but valuable.

Filin wasn't offensive to the eye, either—clean, not large,

wearing an at-home velvet jacket, a small hand weighted down with a ring. And not a clichéd, corny, "ruble fifty with the box" ring—why no, his is straight from an excavation, Venetian if he's not lying, or a setting of a coin from, God help me, Antioch, or something even grander than that. . . . That was Filin. He'll sit in a chair dangling his slipper, fingers folded in a tent, eyebrows like pitch—marvelous Anatolian eyes like soot, a dry silvery beard that rustled, black only around the mouth, as if he had been eating coal.

Plenty to look at.

Filin's women weren't run-of-the-mill, either—collector's rarities. Either a circus performer, say, twisting on a trapeze silvery scales shimmering, to a drum roll; or simply a young woman, a mama's girl who dabbled in water colors, a brain the size of a kopek but dazzlingly white, so that Filin, in issuing his invitation to view, will warn you to bring sunglasses to avoid snow blindness.

Some people privately didn't approve of Filin, with all those rings, pastries, and snuffboxes; they giggled over his raspberry robe with tassels and those supposedly silver Mongol slippers with turned-up noses; and it was funny that in his bathroom he had a special brush for his beard and hand cream: a bachelor . . . But whenever he called, they came; and secretly always worried: would he invite them again? Would he let them sit in the warmth and light, in comfort and luxury, and in general—what did he ever see in us ordinary people, what does he need us for?

"If you're not busy tonight, please come at eight. Meet Alisa, a cha-arming creature."

"Thank you, thank you, of course."

Well, as usual, at the last minute! Yura reached for his razor, and Galya, slithering into her panty hose like a snake, left instructions with her daughter: the kasha is in the pot, don't open the door to anyone, do your homework, and straight to bed. And don't hang on me, let go, we're late already. Galya stuffed plastic bags into her purse: Filin lived in a high-rise, with a grocery store on the ground floor; maybe they'll have herring oil, or something else.

Beyond the house the boundary road lay like a hoop of darkness where the frosty wind howled, the cold of uninhabited plains penetrated your clothes, and the world for a second seemed as horrible as a graveyard; and they didn't want to wait for a bus or be squashed in the metro and they got a taxi; and lounging comfortably, cautiously berated Filin for his velvet jacket, for his collector's passion, for the unknown Alisa: where's the last one, that Ninochka? nowhere to be found now; and wondered whether Matvei Matveich would be there, and roundly denounced Matvei Matveich.

They had met him at Filin's and were charmed by the old man: those stories of his about the reign of Anna Ivanovna and those pastries, and the steam from English tea, and blue-and-gold collector's cups, and Mozart bubbling from somewhere up above, and Filin caressing the guests with his Mephistophelian eyes—and, oh, heads spinning—they got Matvei Matveich to invite them. Some visit! He received them in the kitchen, the floor was made of planks, the walls brown and bare, a horrible neighborhood, nothing but fences and potholes, and he was wearing jogging pants that were thread-bare and the tea was stale and the jam crystallized, and he just thumped the jar on the table, stuck a spoon in it—dig it out yourselves, dear guests. And you had to smoke on the landing: asthma, please understand. And Anna Ivanovna was a flop, too. They sat down—the hell with the tea—to listen to his purring speech about palace intrigues, all kinds of revolts; but the old man kept untying these awful folders and poking them with his finger shouting about land reform and that Kuzin, the

mediocrity clerk backstabber, won't let him get published and
has set the whole department against Matvei Matveich, but
here, here: invaluable documents, he'd been collecting them
all his life. Galya and Yura wanted to hear about villains,
torture, the ice house and the dwarf wedding, but Filin wasn't
there to steer the conversation to interesting topics, and all
they heard that evening was Ku-u-zin! Ku-u-uzin! and the
finger-jabbing of the files, and the valerian sedative drops.
They put the old man to bed and left, and Galya tore her panty
hose on the old man's chair.

"What about Vlasov the bard?" Yura recalled.

"Bite your tongue!"

With him, it was just the opposite; but the shame was
terrible: they picked him up at Filin's, too, and invited him to
their house and invited lots of guests to hear him sing, spent
two hours in line to get a special cake. They locked their
daughter in her room and the dog in the kitchen. Vlasov the
bard came, grim, with his guitar, didn't even try the cake:
cream softens the voice and he wanted his voice hoarse. He
sang a couple of songs: "Aunt Motya, your shoulders, your
pecs and cheeks, like Nadia Comaneci, are developed by
gymnastique. . ." Yura made a fool of himself, showing his
ignorance, loudly whispering in the middle of the song, "I
forget, what part are the pecs?" Galya grew anxious, and, hand
laid on heart in emotion, said he *must* sing "Friends"—it's
such a marvelous, marvelous song. He had sung it at
Filin's—gently, sadly—about "around the table covered with
oilcloth, over a bottle of beer" sit a group of old friends, bald,
all losers. Each one's life went wrong, each has his own sorrow:
"one can't love, the other can't rule"—and no one can help,
alas!—but at least they're together, they're friends, they need
one another, and isn't that the most important thing in life?
You listen and you feel that—yes-yes-yes—the same thing

happened in your life, yes, just like it. "What a song. A hit."
Yura whispered. Vlasov the bard frowned even more, looked
off into the distance—off into that imagined room where the
mutually admiring baldies were uncapping a distant beer; he
strummed the guitar and began sadly, "around the table
covered with oilcloth . . ." Julie, locked in the kitchen,
scratched at the floor and howled. "With a bottle of beer,"
Vlasov continued. *"Woof woof woof,"* the dog persisted. Someone snorted, the bard put his hand on the strings with an
injured air, and took a cigarette. Yura went to deal with Julie.

"Is that autobiographical?" some idiot asked reverently.

"What? All my songs are autobiographical to a degree."

Yura returned, the bard tossed away his butt, and concen-
trated. "Around the table, covered with oilcloth . . ." A
tortured howl came from the kitchen.

"A musical dog," the bard said viciously.

Galya dragged the resisting German shepherd to the
neighbors, the bard hurriedly finished the song—the howling
came through the co-op's walls—he shortened his program,
and then in the foyer as he zipped up his jacket announced
with disgust that he usually charged two rubles a head but
since they didn't know how to organize a creative atmosphere,
he'd settle for a ruble apiece. And Galya ran back to the
neighbors—a nightmare, lend me a ten—and they, also just
before payday, dug around, collecting change and shaking the
kids' piggy bank to the howls of the robbed children and the
barking of overjoyed Julie.

Yes, Filin knows how to deal with people, and we sure
don't. Well, maybe next time it'll go better.

It wasn't quite eight yet—just enough time to stand in line
for pâté in the store at the bottom of the block of flats where
Filin lived. There's no trouble finding cows in our suburb, but
you just try finding pâté. At three minutes to eight they got

into the elevator, and Galya, as usual, looked around and said, "I could live in an elevator like this," then the polished parquet floor of the landing, the brass plate: "I. I. Filin," the bell; and then the man himself on the doorstep, black eyes glowing, head tilted to one side: "Punctuality is the politeness of princes . . ."

And it's so pleasant hearing that, those words, as if Filin were a sultan and they truly were princes, Galya in her inexpensive coat and Yura in his jacket and knit cap.

And they floated in, the royal pair, chosen for one evening, into the warmth and light, the sweet piano trills, and proceeded to the table where the hothouse roses refuse to acknowledge the frost, wind, darkness that have besieged Filin's impregnable tower, powerless to penetrate.

Something elusive is different in the apartment . . . ah, they see: the glass case with the beaded trifles has been moved, the candelabra has moved to the other wall, the arch leading to the back room is curtained, and moving that curtain aside . . . Alisa, the allegedly charming creature, comes out and offers her hand.

"Allochka."

"Well, yes, she is Allochka, but we will call her Alisa, isn't that right? Please, sit down," said Filin. "Well, I recommend the pâté. A rarity. You know, pâtés like this . . ."

"I see you got it downstairs," Yura said happily. " 'We go down. From the conquered heights. Even the gods descended'—isn't that how it goes?"

Filin smiled thinly and twitched an eyebrow—to say maybe I got it downstairs and maybe I didn't. You have to know everything, don't you? Galya mentally kicked her husband for his tactlessness.

"Appreciate the tartlets," Filin started anew. "I'm afraid that you are the last people to have them on this sinful earth."

Tonight he called the pirozhki "tartlets" for some reason—
probably because of Alisa.

"Why, what happened, have they stopped selling flour? On
a global scale?" Yura was in good humor, rubbing his hands,
his bony nose red in the heat. The tea gurgled.

"Nothing of the kind. What is flour?" Filin's beard nodded.
"Some sugar, Galya. . . . What is flour? The secret is lost, my
friends. The last person to know the ancient recipe is dying—I
just got a call. Ninety-eight, a stroke. Try them, Alisa; may
I pour you tea in my favorite cup?"

Filin's gaze grew misty, as if hinting at the possibilities of
special closeness that could result from such intimate contact
with his beloved dishes. The charming Alisa smiled. What
was so charming about her? Her black hair shone as if it were
greased, a hook nose, mustache. Simple dress, knit, the color
of a pickle. Big deal. Better women than she have sat here, and
where were they now?

"And just think," Filin was saying. "Just two days ago I
ordered the tartlets from this Ignaty Kirillych. Just yesterday
he baked them. Just this morning I got them, each wrapped
in tissue paper. And now, a stroke. They called me from
Sklifosovsky hospital." Filin bit into a puff pastry bomb,
raised his handsome brows, and sighed.

"When still a lad, Ignaty worked at the Yar, and the old
pastry chef Kuzma gave him the secret of these pastries on his
deathbed. Just try them." Filin wiped his beard. "And Kuzma
had worked in Petersburg in his day at Wolf and Beranger—
the famous pastry shop. They say that before his fatal duel,
Pushkin dropped by Wolf's and asked for tartlets. That day
Kuzma was sleeping off a binge and hadn't baked any. Well,
the manager said, we don't have any. These people are like
that, Alexander Sergeyevich. Wouldn't you like a bouchée? Or
a cream horn? Pushkin got upset, waved his hat, and left.

Well, you know what happened later. Kuzma overslept, and Pushkin is in his grave."

"Oh, my god," said Galya.

"Oh, yes. And do you know it had repercussions on everyone? Wolf shot himself. Beranger converted to Russian Orthodoxy, the manager donated thirty thousand to a religious institution, and Kuzma simply lost his mind. He kept muttering, 'Oh, Alexander Sergeyevich. . . . You didn't have my tartlets . . . If only you had waited a bit . . .' "

Filin tossed another pirozhok in his mouth and crunched. "However, that Kuzma lived to our day. He passed on the recipe to his students with shaking hands. Ignaty got the dough; someone else, the filling. Well, then came the revolution, the civil war. The one who knew the filling joined the Social Revolutionaries. Ignaty lost track of him. A few years later—Ignaty was still with the restaurant—something prompted him, he came out of the kitchen, and there at a table is that man with a lady. He's got a monocle, a mustache—unrecognizable. Ignaty runs over to him as is, covered with flour. 'Come with me, comrade.' The man had no choice. White as a sheet, into the kitchen he went. 'Bastard, tell me the meat filling.' What could he do, his past could cause him trouble. He told. 'Tell me the cabbage filling.' He trembled, but he did it. 'And now the fish.' That was absolutely top secret. He said nothing. Ignaty: 'The fish!' And he picked up his rolling pin. The man said nothing. Then suddenly he screamed and ran out. They chased him, tied him up, and looked at him—he'd lost his mind, he was rolling his eyes and foaming at the mouth. So the fish remained a secret. Yes . . . That Ignaty Kirillych was an interesting old man, so fastidious. How he felt puff pastry, what a feel for it! . . . He baked at home. He'd draw the curtains, double lock the door. I would say, 'Ignaty Kirillych, dear man, share your secret, what's it to you?' but he wouldn't budge. He kept waiting for a worthy recipient. And now the stroke . . . Try one."

"Oh, I'm so sorry," the charming Alisa said. "How can I eat them now? I'm always so sorry for the last of anything. . . . My mother had a brooch before the war. . . ."

"The last one, an accidental one!" sighed Filin and took another pirozhok.

"The last storm cloud," Galya entered the game.

"The last of the Mohicans," added Yura.

"No, my mother had this pearl brooch before the war. . . ."

"Everything is transitory, dear Alisa," Filin said, chewing in satisfaction. "Everything ages—dogs, women, pearls. Let us sigh over the fleeting nature of existence and thank the creator for giving us a chance to taste this and that at the feast of life. Eat and wipe your tears."

"Perhaps he'll regain consciousness, that Ignaty?"

"He can't," the host assured them. "Forget about it."

They chewed. Music sang overhead. It was good.

"What new pleasures do you have?" Yura asked.

"Ah . . . I'm glad you reminded me. Wedgwood—cups and saucers. Creamer. See, blue on the shelf. Why I'll just . . . Here . . ."

"Ah . . ." Galya touched the cup carefully with her finger—white carefree dances on a blue foggy meadow.

"Do you like it, Alisa?"

"Nice . . . Now before the war my mother had . . ."

"Do you know where I got it? Guess . . . From a partisan."

"In what sense?"

"Just listen. It's a curious story." Filin made a tent with his fingers and looked lovingly at the shelf where the captive service sat cautiously, afraid of falling. "I was wandering around villages this fall with a rifle. I stopped by one hut. A man brought out some fresh milk for me. In a cup. I look—it's real Wedgwood. How could it be? Well, we got to talking, his name is Uncle Sasha, I have the address somewhere . . . well, it doesn't matter. Here's what I learned. During the war he was a partisan in the woods. Early morning. German plane flying over. *Bzzzzzzz,*" Filin added an imitation. "Uncle Sasha looked up just when the pilot spat—right in his face. An accident, of course. But Uncle Sasha's temper flared, naturally, he went *bang* with his gun—and hit the German. Also accidentally. The plane fell, they looked inside—five crates of cocoa, and the sixth had these dishes. He must have been delivering breakfast. I bought the set. The creamer is cracked, but that's all right. Considering the circumstances."

"Your partisan is a liar." Yura was delighted, he looked around and slapped his thigh. "What a great liar. Fantastic!"

"Nothing of the sort." Filin was not pleased. "Of course, I can't rule out that he's no partisan at all but just a vulgar little thief, but you know . . . somehow I prefer to believe."

He grew huffy and took the cup back.

"Of course, you have to believe people." Galya stepped on Yura's foot under the table. "An amazing thing happened to me, too. Remember, Yura? I bought a wallet, brought it home, and inside were three rubles. No one believes it."

"Why not, I believe it. It happens," Alisa mused. "Now, my mother . . ."

They talked about the amazing, about premonitions, and dreams. Alisa had a girlfriend who had predicted her entire life ahead of time—marriage, two children, divorce, division of the apartment and property. Yura told in great detail how a friend's car was stolen and how the police cleverly figured the thief's identity and caught him, but the real trick was—he couldn't remember it right now. Filin described a dog he knew that unlocked the door with its own key and heated up dinner for its masters.

"Really, how?" the women gasped.

"Easily. They have a French oven, electric, with a control panel. Push a button, everything goes on. The dog looks at the time: goes to the kitchen, works there; well, warms something up for itself, too. The owners come home from work and the soup is on the boil, the bread sliced, the table set. Convenient."

Filin talked, smiled, turned his ankle, glanced over at satisfied Alisa, the music died down, and the city made itself heard through the windows. Dark tea steamed in their cups, sweet cigarette smoke curled upward, the roses gave off their scent and beyond the window the Sadovoye Ring Road quietly squealed beneath tires and people cheerfully plowed through the streets, the city glowed in wreaths of golden street lamps, frosty rainbow rings, multicolored crunchy snow, while the capital's sky sowed new charming snow, fresh, just made. And just think, this entire feast, this evening of miracles was created especially for this completely unspecial Allochka, extravagantly renamed Alisa—there she sat in her vegetable dress, mustached mouth open, delightedly staring at the all-powerful gentleman who with a wave of the hand, the flicker of an eyebrow can transform the world to the point of unrecognizability.

Soon Galya and Yura would leave, crawling back to their outskirts, and she would stay, she was allowed. . . . Galya grew depressed. Why, oh, why?

Filin's tower nestled in the middle of the capital, a pink mountain, ornamented here and there in the most varied way—with all sorts of architectural doodads, thingamajigs, and whatnots: there were towers on the socles, crenels on the towers, and ribbons and wreaths between the crenellations, and out of the laurel garlands peeked a book, the source of knowledge, or a compass stuck out its pedagogic leg; or, if you looked, you'd see a puffy obelisk in the middle, and standing firmly on it, embracing a sheaf, a firm plaster woman with a clear gaze that rebuffs storms and night, with flawless braids and an innocent chin. . . . You kept expecting trumpets to sound and drums to play something governmental and heroic.

And the evening sky above Filin and his curlicued palace plays with light—brick, lilac—a real Moscow, theatrical sky.

While back in their outskirts . . . oh my God it'll be nothing but thick oily cold darkness, empty in the cool abysses between houses, you can't even see the houses, they've blended into the night sky weighted down by snow clouds with an occasional window burning in an uneven pattern: gold, green, red squares struggling to push aside the polar murk. . . . It's late, the stores are locked and bolted, the last old lady has rolled out, carrying a packet of margarine and an eggbeater, no one is walking along the streets just for the fun of it, no one is looking around, strolling; everyone has slipped into his own door, drawn the curtains, and is reaching for the TV knob. If you look out the window, you see the boundary road, an abyss of darkness marked by doubled red lights and the yellow beetles of someone's headlights. . . . Something big drove by, its lights nodding in a pothole. . . . Here comes a stick of light—the headlights in the bus's forehead, a trembling nucleus of yellow light, live roe of people inside. . . . And beyond the regional road, beyond the last weak strip of life, on the other side of the snow-filled ravine, the invisible sky slipped down, resting its heavy edge on a beet field—right there, on the other side of the ravine. It was impossible, unthinkable, unbearable to realize that the thick darkness extended farther, over the fields that blended into a white roar, over badly constructed fences, over trees pressed into the cold earth where a doomed dull light quivers as if held in an indifferent fist . . . and farther once again, the dark white cold, a crust of forest where the darkness is even thicker, where perhaps a pathetic wolf is forced to live: it comes out on a hill in its rough wool coat smelling of juniper and blood, wildness, disaster, gazes grimly and with disgust at the blind windy vistas, clumps of snow hardening between its cracked claws, and its teeth are gritted in sadness, and a cold tear hangs like a stinking bead on the furry cheek, and everyone is the enemy and everyone is the killer. . . .

For dessert they had pineapple. And then they had to get out. And it was so far to the house. . . . Avenues, avenues, avenues, dark blizzardy squares, deserted lots, bridges and forests, and more lots, and unexpected not-sleeping factories, light blue inside, and more forests and the snow in the headlights. And at home—boring green wallpaper, the cut-glass lamp fixture in the foyer, the dull cramped feeling and the familiar smell, and the color cover of a woman's magazine tacked to the wall for decoration. A rosy, disgusting couple on skis. She's grinning, he's warming her hands. *"Chilled?"* it's called. "Chilled?" She'd tear it off the wall, but Yura won't let her, he likes things sporty, optimistic. . . . So let him find a taxi.

Night had entered the deep hours, all the gates were closed, joyriding trucks zipped by, the starry ceiling hardened with the cold. The rough air had formed into clumps. "Hey, chief, take us to the city line?" Yura ran from car to car. Galya whimpered and switched from foot to foot, hopping on the side of the road, and behind her, in the palace, the last lights were going out, the roses plunging into sleep, Alisa babbling about her mother's brooch, while Filin, in his tasseled robe, tickled her with his silvery beard: Ooh, darling. More pineapple?

That winter they were invited once more, and Allochka hung around the apartment as if she belonged there, bravely grabbing the expensive dishes and smelling of lily of the valley and yawning.

Filin demonstrated Valtasarov to his guests—a dreamy bearded muzhik, amazing in his ventriloquism skills. Valtasarov could imitate a knock at the door, a cow being milked, the rattle of a wagon, the distant howl of wolves, and a woman killing cockroaches. He couldn't do industrial sounds. Yura begged him to try, to at least do a trolley, but he refused flat out: " 'Fraid of busting my gut." Galya was uncomfortable: she sensed in Valtasarov the degree of noncivilization from which she and Yura were a stone's throw—over the city line, beyond the ravine, to the other side.

She must have gotten weary of late. . . . Just six months ago she would have actively pursued Valtasarov, invited him and a group of friends, served cracked sugar, rye cakes, and radishes—and whatever else the old peasant liked to eat—and he would have mooed and rattled the well chain to general excitement. But now it suddenly was clear to her: it wouldn't work. If she were to invite him, the guests would laugh and leave, but Valtasarov would stay, ask to spend the night, probably—and she'd have to clear the room, and it was right in the middle of the apartment; he'd go to bed around nine or something, and it would smell of sheep, and shag, and haylofts; at night he'd stumble to the kitchen in the dark for a drink of water and knock over a chair. . . . A quiet curse. Julie would start barking, their daughter would wake up. . . . Or maybe he was a lunatic and would come into their bedroom in the dark . . . in a white shirt and felt boots . . . rummaging. . . . And in the morning, when you don't feel like seeing anyone at all, when you're in a hurry to get to work and your hair's a mess and it's cold—the old man would sit in the kitchen making a production of having tea, and then pull out illiterate scraps of paper from his pocket: "Girl, they wrote down this medicine for me. . . . It cures everything. . . . How can I get it?"

No, no, no! Don't even think about getting involved with him.

It was only Filin, untiring, who was capable of picking up, feeding, and amusing anyone at all—well, including us, too, of course! Oh, Filin! Generous owner of golden fruit, he hands them out right and left, giving food to the hungry and drink to the thirsty; he waves his hand, and gardens bloom, women grow more beautiful, bores get inspired, and crows sing like nightingales.

That's what he's like. That's him.

And what marvelous friends he has. . . . Ignaty Kirillych, the pastry wizard. Or that ballerina he visits—Doltseva-Elanskaya . . .

"Of course, that's her stage name," said Filin, kicking his foot and admiring the ceiling. "Her maiden name was Dogina, Olga Ieronimovna. Her first husband was Katkin, the second Mousekin. A game of diminishing returns, so to speak. She was quite a hit in her day. Grand dukes stood in line, bringing her topazes by the sack. That was her weakness, smoky topazes. But she was a very simple, heartfelt, progressive woman. After the revolution she decided to give her stones to the people. She was as good as her word: she took off her necklace, tore the thread, poured them out on the table. There was a knock at the door: they came to move more people into her apartment. While they talked and so on, by the time she came back the parrot had eaten them all. Birds, as you know, need stones for their digestion. He'd devoured about five millions' worth—and he flew out the window. She followed. 'Kokosha, where are you going? What about the people?' He went south. She followed. She reached Odessa, don't ask me how. The ship was taking off, the stacks smoking, shouts, suitcases—people fleeing to Constantinople. The parrot landed on the smokestack and sat there. He was warm. So this Olga Dogina, what do you think, she hooked her trained leg over the side of the ship and stopped the ship. And she wouldn't let go until they got her the parrot. She shook everything out of it down to the last kopek and donated it to the Red Cross. Of course, they had to amputate her leg, but she didn't give up, she danced in hospitals on crutches. Now she's hundreds of years old, flat on her back, put on weight. I visit her, read Sterne to her. Yes, Olga Dogina, from a merchant family . . . Think what power there is in our people. So much untapped power . . ."

Galya regarded Filin with adoration. Suddenly he was clear to her—handsome, giving, hospitable . . . Oh, how lucky that mustachioed Allochka was. She didn't appreciate him, turning her indifferent lemur-shiny eyes at the guests, Filin, the flowers and cookies, as if this were the usual order of things, as if this is just the way things should be. As if far away at the ends of the earth, Galya's daughter, dog, and "Chilled?" were not languishing, hostages in the dark on the threshold of the aspen forest, quivering with rage.

For dessert they had grapefruit stuffed with shrimp, and the magical old man drank tea from his saucer.

A stone lay on her heart.

At home, in the darkness, listening to the glassy ringing of the aspens, the roar of the sleepless boundary road, the rustles of wolf fur in the distant forest, the slither of the chilled beet greens under their snow blanket, she thought: we'll never get out of here. Someone unnamed, indifferent, like fate, had decided: this one, this one, and this one will live in a palace. Life will be good for them. And these, and these, and these ones, too, including Galya and Yura, will live there. No, not there, wa-a-ay over there, that's right, yes. By the ravine, beyond the deserted lots. And don't be pushy, don't bother. End of conversation. Wait a minute! What is this? But fate has already turned its back, laughing with its friends, and its iron back is solid—you can't get its attention by knocking. If you want, you can have hysterics, roll on the floor, kick your legs, if you want, you can lie low and gradually turn wild, collecting portions of cold poison in your teeth.

They tried clambering, tried switching, posting notices, turned the apartment exchange newsletter into Swiss cheese, gutting it, telephoned in humiliation: "We have a forest . . . wonderful air . . . it's great for the child, and you don't need a dacha . . . same to you. You're nuts!" They filled notebooks with hurried notations: "Zinaida Samoilovna is thinking it over. . . ." "Hana will call back. . . ." "Peter Ivanych has to have a balcony. . . ." Miraculously, Yura found an old woman who had a three-room apartment on the second floor in Patriarshie Prudy, in the middle of Moscow, and she was willful and spoiled. Fifteen families got entangled in an exchange chain, each with its own demands, heart attacks, crazy neighbors, broken hearts, and lost birth certificates. They taxied the capricious old woman hither and yon, got expensive medications for her, as well as warm boots and ham, and promised her money. It was on the verge of happening, thirty-eight people trembled and grumbled, weddings were called off, summer vacations burst, somewhere in the chain a certain Simakov dropped out, bleeding ulcers—doesn't matter, forget him—the ranks closed, more efforts, the old woman equivocated and resisted, under horrible pressure signed the documents, and just at the moment when somewhere in the cloudy skies a pink angel filled out the order with an air pen, *bam!* she changed her mind. Just like that—upped and changed it. And just leave her alone.

The howl of fifteen families shook the earth, the axis shifted, volcanoes erupted, Hurricane Anna wiped out a young underdeveloped nation, the Himalayas grew even taller and the Marianas Trench deeper, but Galya and Yura remained where they were. And the wolves giggled in the forest. For it was written: if you are meant to chirp, don't purr. If you are meant to purr, don't chirp.

"Should we denounce the old woman?" Galya said.

"But to whom?" Haggard Yura burned with an evil flame, it was sad to look at him. He figured this and that—no go. Maybe complain to St. Peter, so that he wouldn't let the lousy woman into Heaven. Yura picked up a lot of rocks in the quarry and went one night to her house to break her windows, but came back with the news that they were broken—they weren't the only ones with the bright idea.

Then they cooled off, of course.

Now she lay and thought about Filin: how he folded his fingers into a tent, smiled, dangled his foot, how he raised his eyes to the ceiling when he talked. . . . There was so much she had to tell him. . . . Bright light, bright flowers, the bright silvery beard with the black spot around his mouth. Of course, Alisa was no match for him, and she couldn't appreciate the wonderland. Nor did she deserve it. He needed someone understanding. . . .

"Blah-blah-blah," said Yura in his sleep.

. . . Yes, someone understanding and sensitive . . . to steam his raspberry robe . . . run his bath . . . do something with his slippers . . .

They'd divide their property like this: Yura could have the apartment, the dog, and the furniture. Galya would take their daughter, some of the linens, the iron, and the washing

machine. The toaster. The mirror from the hallway. Mother's
good forks. The African violet. That's all, probably.

No, that's nonsense. How could you understand Galya's
life, Galya's third-rate existence, the humiliation, the jabs at
her soul? How can you describe it? How can you describe—
well, how about the time Galya managed to get—through
chicanery, bribery, and the necessary phone calls—a ticket to
the Bolshoi—in the orchestra!—just one lousy ticket (of
course, Yura wasn't interested in culture), how she bathed,
steamed, and curled herself, preparing for the big event, how
she left the house on tiptoe, cherishing the golden atmosphere
of the lofty and beautiful in herself—but it was autumn, it
started to pour, and she couldn't get a taxi, and Galya rushed
around in the slush, damning the skies, fate, the city builders,
and when she finally got to the theater she realized she had left
her good shoes at home and her boots were full of mud and the
soles had red cakes with clumps of grass sticking out of
them—a vulgar bumpkin, a country creep, a local yokel. Even
the hem of her dress was messed up.

So Galya—and what was so bad about that?—simply crept
to the ladies' room quietly and washed her boots with her
hankie and rinsed off the shameful hem. And then this
toad—not an employee, but an art lover—like lilac jelly, her
cameos jiggling, started in on her: How dare you! At the
Bolshoi, scraping your filthy feet, you're not in a bathhouse,
you know! And she went on and on and people started to stare
and whisper and, not knowing what was going on, to give her
dirty looks.

And it was ruined for her, spoiled and lost, and Galya
wasn't up to high drama, and the small swans wasted their
famous dance at a slow canter. Angry tears boiling, tormented
by unavenged injury, Galya flattened the dancers with her gaze
without any pleasure, making out through her binoculars their

yellowish working faces, their laboring neck muscles, and severely, ruthlessly told herself that they weren't swans at all but union members, that their lives were like everyone else's—ingrown toenails, unfaithful husbands—and that as soon as they finished their dance, they would pull on warm knit pants and head for home, for home: in icy Zyuzino, and puddly Korovino, and even to that horrible city limits road where Galya howled silently at night, into that impenetrable misery where you can only run and croak inhumanly. And let's see that white insouciant fluttery one, *that* one, take Galya's daily path, let her fall belly-deep into the tortuous mud, in the viscous Precambrian of the outskirts, and let's see her twist and clamber out—now, *that* would be some *fouetté.*

How can you describe that?

In March he didn't call, and in April he didn't call, and the summer passed in vain, and Galya was going crazy: What was wrong? Was he sick of them? Were they unworthy? She was tired of dreaming, of waiting for the phone call, she began to forget the beloved features: now she pictured him as a giant, frightening black gaze, huge hands with sparkling rings, dry, oriental beard with a metallic rustle.

And she didn't recognize him right away when he passed her in the subway—small, hurrying, careworn—he went around her without noticing and just walked on, and it was too late to hail him.

He walked like an ordinary man; his small feet, accustomed to polished parquet, spoiled by velvet slippers, stepped on the spittle-covered bathroom tiles of the passageway, ran up the ordinary steps; small fists rummaged in pockets, located a handkerchief, hit his nose—*boof, boof!*—and back in the pocket; then he shook himself like a dog, adjusted his scarf, and went on, under the archway with faded gold mosaics, past the statue of a partisan patriarch, confusedly spreading his bronze hand with an annoying error in the position of his fingers.

He walked through the crowd, and the crowd, thickening and thinning, rustled, pushed against him—a cheerful over-weight woman, an amber Hindu in snow white Muslim underpants, a soldier with boils, old mountain women in galoshes, stunned by the bustle.

He walked without looking back, he had no time for Galya, her greedy eyes, extended neck—he leaped up like a schoolboy and onto the escalator—and he was gone, vanished, no more, only the warm rubber wind from an approaching train, the hiss and bang of the doors, and the speech of the crowd like the speech of many waters.

And that same evening Allochka called and informed her indignantly that she and Filin went to get married and there, filling out the forms, she discovered he was a pretender, that he was subletting the apartment in the high-rise from some polar explorer, and all those things probably belong to the explorer and not to him, and that he was actually registered as living in the town of Domodedovo. And that she proudly threw the papers at him and left, not because of Domodedovo, of course, but because her pride wouldn't let her marry a man who had lied to her even this much. And they should know whom they're dealing with.

So that was it. . . . And they had associated with him. Why he was no better than they, he was just like them, he was simply pretending, mimicking, that pathetic midget, that clown in a shah's robe.

Even on the landing she could smell the boiled fish. Galya rang the bell, Filin opened the door and was astonished. He was alone and looked terrible, worse than Julie. Tell him everything. Why stand on ceremony? He was alone and was brazenly eating cod and listening to Brahms, and he had

placed a vase with white carnations on the table in front of
him.

"Galochka, what a surprise. You haven't forgotten me. . . .
Please, have some perch Orly, it's fresh." Filin offered
the cod.

"I know everything," Galya said and sat down, as is, in her
coat. "Alisa told me everything."

"Yes, Alisa, Alisa, what a treacherous woman. Well, how
about the fish?"

"No, thank you. And I know about Domodedovo. And
about the polar explorer."

"Yes, a horrible story," Filin said sadly. "The man spent
three years in the Antarctic and he'd still be there—it's
romantic—and for such a thing to happen to him. But Dr.
Ilizarov will be able to help, I'm sure of it. They do that here."

"Do what?" Galya was bewildered.

"Ears. Don't you know? My explorer froze off his ears. He's
a Siberian, expansive and generous, they were having an
International Women's Day party with some Norwegians, and
one Norwegian liked his fur cap with ear flaps, and so he
traded with him. For a cap. It was eighty below outside and
seventy degrees indoors. That's a hundred fifty degree difference, can you imagine? Someone called his name from the
street: 'Petya!' he stuck out his head, and his ears—wham!—
just fell off. Of course, there was general panic, they hauled
him over the coals, stuck his ears in a box, and flew him
immediately to Kurgan, to Dr. Ilizarov. So here's what . . .
I'm leaving."

Galya sought words in vain. Something painful.

"Really," sighed Filin. "It's autumn. It's sad. Everyone's
abandoned me. Alisa abandoned me. . . . Matvei Matveich
hasn't shown his nose. . . . Maybe he's dead? You're the only
one, Galochka. . . . You're the only one who could, if you

wanted to. But now I'll be closer to you. I'll be closer now.
Have some perch. *Einmal in der Woche, Fisch,* which means,
fish once a week. Who said that? Well, which famous person
said that?"

"Goethe?" Galya muttered, softening against her will.

"Close. Close, but not quite." Filin was animated and
younger. "We're forgetting our history of literature, tsk-
tsk-tsk. . . . I'll give you a hint: when Goethe—you were
right there—was an old man, he fell in love with the young
and charming Ulrike. He was foolish enough to offer
his hand and was cruelly refused. From the doorway. Rather,
from the window. The beauty stuck her head out the window
and berated the Olympian—well, you know all that, you
have to know. You're old, and so on. A real Faust. You
should eat more fish—it has phosphorus to make your brain
work. *Einmal in der Woche, Fisch.* And she slammed the
window."

"No!" Galya said. "But why . . . I've read . . ."

"We've all read something, my dear," Filin said, blooming. "I'm giving you the bare facts." He sat more comfortably
and raised his eyes to the ceiling. "So the old man wanders
home, shattered. As they say, farewell, Antonina Petrovna,
my unsung song. . . . He was stooped, the star on his neck
went jingle jangle, jingle jangle. . . . It's evening, dinner
time. They serve game with peas. He loved game, I hope
you're not going to argue with that? The candles were lit,
silverware on the table, you know, the German kind with
knobs, and the aroma. . . . So, the children were there, and
the grandchildren there. And in the corner, his secretary,
Eckerman, settled in, writing. Goethe picked on a wing and
tossed it aside. He couldn't eat it. Nor the peas. The
grandchildren say, Gramps, what's the matter? He got up,
threw his chair down, and said bitterly: once a week, she says,

eat fish. He burst into tears and left. The Germans are sentimental. Eckerman, of course, put it all down. If you haven't had a chance, read *Conversations with Goethe*. An edifying book. By the way, they used to exhibit that game bird—absolutely petrified by then—in a museum in Weimar, until 1932."

"What did they do with the peas?" Galya asked furiously.

"Fed them to the cat."

"Since when do cats eat vegetables?"

"Just try not eating them with the Germans. They have discipline."

"What, did Eckerman write about the cat too?"

"Yes, it's in the notes. Depends on the edition, of course."

Galya got up, left, went downstairs and outside. Farewell, pink palace, farewell, my dream. Go fly in all four directions, Filin! We stood with arms extended—to whom? What did you give us? Your tree with golden fruits has dried up and your words are just fireworks in the night, a moment's run of colored zephyrs, the hysteria of fiery roses in the dark over our hair.

It was getting dark. The autumn wind toyed with papers, scooping them out of the bins. She looked for the last time into the store that had undermined the palace's foot like a worm. She stood near the unhappy counters—veal bones, "Dawn" mashed potatoes. Well, let's wipe our tears with a finger, smear them on our cheeks, let's spit at the votive lights: our god is dead and his temple is empty. Farewell.

And now, home. The path is far. Ahead is a new winter, new hopes, new songs. Well, let's sing the praises of the outskirts, the rains, the grayed houses, the long evenings on the threshold of darkness. Let's sing the praises of the deserted lots, the grayish grasses, the cold of the mud under cautious feet, let's sing the slow autumn dawn, the barking dogs amid aspens, the fragile golden gossamer webs, and the first ice, the first bluish ice with a deep imprint of someone else's foot.

PETERS

Even as a child, Peters had flat feet and a woman's broad belly. His late grandmother, who loved him as he was, taught him good manners—chew every little bit thoroughly, tuck your napkin under your chin, and be quiet when adults are talking. So his grandmother's friends all liked him. When she took him visiting with her, he could safely be allowed to touch an expensive book with illustrations—he wouldn't tear it—and at the table he never pulled the fringe from the tablecloth or crumbled his cookies—a wonderful boy. They liked the way he entered, too, tugging down his jacket in a dignified manner, adjusting his bow tie or lace jabot, as yellowed as his grandmother's cheeks; and clicking the heels of his flat feet, he

would introduce himself to the old ladies using the old
Russian "s" (a contraction for "sir") at the end of his name.
"Peter-s!" He noticed that amused and touched them.

"Ah, Petya, child! So you call him *Peter,* do you?"

"Yes . . . well . . . we're studying German now," his
grandmother would say casually. And reflected in dull mirrors,
Peters walked in measured tread down the hallway, past old
trunks, past old smells, into rooms where rag dolls sat in
corners, where green cheese dreamt under a green cover on the
table and homemade cookies gave off a vanilla aroma. While
the hostess put out the small silver spoons, corroded on one
side, Peters wandered around the room, examining the dolls
on the chest, the portrait of the severe, offended old man with
a mustache like a long spoke, the vignettes on the wallpaper,
or approached the window and looked through the thickets of
aloe out into the sunny cold air where blue pigeons flew and
rosy-cheeked children sledded down tracked hills. He wasn't
allowed to go outside.

The stupid nickname Peters stuck the rest of his life.

Peters's mother, Grandmother's daughter, ran off to warmer
climes with a scoundrel, his father spent time with loose
women and took no interest in his son. Listening to the
grownups' conversation, Peters pictured the scoundrel as a
Negro under a banana palm and Father's women as light blue
and airy, floating around untethered like spring clouds; but,
well brought up by his grandmother, he said nothing. Besides
a grandmother, he also had a grandfather who used to lie
quietly in the corner in a armchair, saying nothing and
watching Peters with shining glassy eyes, then they laid him
out on the dining room table, kept him there for two days and
then took him away. They had rice porridge that day.

Grandmother promised Peters that if he behaved, he would
live marvelously when he grew up. Peters said nothing. In the

evenings, in bed with his fuzzy bunny, he described his future life to it—how he would go out whenever he felt like it, play with all the kids, how Mama and the scoundrel would come visit and bring him sweet fruits, how father's loose women would float around with him, as if in a dream. The bunny believed him.

His grandmother gave Peters slapdash German lessons. They played the very old game, Black Peter, drawing cards from each other's hand and matching up pairs—goose and gander, rooster and hen, dogs with haughty faces. Only the cat, Black Peter, had no pair, he was always alone—grim and withdrawn—and whoever got stuck with Black Peter at the end of the game lost and just sat there like a fool.

They also had color postcards with captions: Wiesbaden, Karlsruhe; there were transparent inserts without feathers but with a window: if you look into the window, you see someone distant, tiny, on horseback. They also sang "O Tannenbaum, O Tannenbaum!" All that was German lessons.

When Peters turned six, his grandmother took him to a New Year's party. The children had been checked out: not infectious. Peters walked as fast as he could in the snow, his grandmother barely kept up. His throat was snugly wrapped in a white scarf, his eyes shone in the dark like a cat's. He was in a hurry to make friends. The marvelous life was beginning. The big hot apartment smelled of pine, toys and stars sparkled, other people's mothers bustled with pies and soft pretzels, quick, agile children squealed and raced around. Peters stopped in the middle of the room and waited for them to make friends. "Catch us, tubby!" they shouted. Peters ran blindly and then stopped. They smashed into him, he fell and stood up, like a weighted doll. Hard adult hands moved him toward the wall. He stood there until tea was served.

At tea all the children behaved badly except Peters. He ate

his portion, wiped his mouth, and awaited events, but there were no events. Only one girl, as black as a beetle, asked him if he had any warts and showed him hers.

Peters immediately fell in love with the girl with the warts and dogged her every step. He asked her to sit on the couch with him and that no one else come near her. But he couldn't wiggle his ears or roll his tongue into a tube, which she requested, and she quickly grew bored and abandoned him. Then he didn't know what to do. Then he wanted to spin in place and shout loudly, and he spun and shouted, and then his grandmother was dragging him home through blue snow banks saying indignantly that she simply didn't recognize him, that he was all sweaty and that they would no longer visit children. And in fact, they were never there again.

Until he was fifteen, Peters held his grandmother's hand when they walked on the street. First she supported him and then vice versa. At home they played dominoes and solitaire. Peters used a jigsaw. He wasn't a good student. Before dying, his grandmother got Peters into a library school and willed him to protect his throat and wash his hands thoroughly.

The day she was buried the ice broke on the Neva River.

In the library where Peters worked, the women were not attractive. And he liked attractive women. But what could he offer such a woman, if he ever met one? A pink belly and tiny eyes? If only he were a brilliant conversationalist, if only he knew German well; but no, all he remembered from his childhood was Karlsruhe. But in his imagination he has an affair with a gorgeous woman. While she does this and that, he reads Schiller out loud to her. In the original. Or Hölderlin. She doesn't understand a word, naturally, nor

could she, but that's not important; what's important is how
he reads—with inspiration, with a musical ripple in his
voice. . . . Holding the book close to his nearsighted eyes . . .
No, no, of course he'll get contact lenses. Though they say
they pinch. So, here he is reading. "Drop the book," she says.
Kisses, tears, and the dawn, the dawn . . . And the contacts
pinch. He'll blink and squint and poke his fingers in his
eyes. . . . She'll wait a bit and then say, "Just peel those
damned bits of glass off, good lord!" And get up and slam the
door.

No. This is better. A sweet, quiet blonde. Her head on his
shoulder. He is reading Hölderlin out loud. Maybe Schiller.
Dark forests, mermaids . . . He's reading and reading, his
mouth is dried out. She'll yawn and say, "Good lord, how long
am I supposed to listen to this stuff?"

No, that wouldn't do, either.

What if he left out the German? Without the German, it
could go something like this: a knockout woman, like a
leopard. And he's like a tiger. Have to have ostrich feathers, a
lithe silhouette on the couch. . . . (Have it slipcovered.) The
silhouette, then. The cushions fall to the floor. And the dawn,
the dawn . . . Maybe I'll even marry her. Why not? Peters
looked at his reflection in the mirror, the fat nose, the eyes
rolling with passion, the soft flat feet. And so what? He looked
a bit like a polar bear, women ought to like that and be
pleasantly frightened. Peters blew at himself in the mirror to
cool off. But neither friendships nor affairs happened.

Peters tried going to dances, stumbling about, panting, and
stepping on young ladies' feet: he would approach a group of
laughing and chatting people, clasp his hands behind his back,
tilt his head to one side, and listen to the conversation. It was
getting dark, August was blowing cool air from the stiff
bushes, sprinkling the red dust of the last rays over the black
foliage and the park's paths; lights went on in the stalls and

kiosks selling wine and meat, and Peters went past severely, holding on to his wallet, but unable to resist the wave of hunger that engulfed him, bought a half dozen pastries, went off to the side, and in the gathered darkness hurriedly consumed them from the glinting metal plate. When he came out of the darkness, blinking, licking his lips, with white cream on his chin, and mustered his courage, he approached people and introduced himself—blindly, headlong, seeing nothing out of fear, clicking the heels of his flat feet—and women recoiled and men intended to punch him, but took a closer look and changed their minds.

No one wanted to play with him.

At home Peters beat egg yolks and sugar for his throat, washed and dried the glass, then set his slippers neatly on the bedside rug, got into bed, stretching his arms out on top of the covers, and lay motionless, staring into the twilit, pulsating ceiling until sleep came for him.

Sleep came, invited him into its loopholes and corridors, made dates on secret stairways, locked the doors and rebuilt familiar houses, frightening him with trunks and women and bubonic plagues and black diamonds, quickly led him along dark passages, and pushed him into a stuffy room where a man sat at a table twiddling his thumbs, shaggy and laughing mockingly, knowledgeable in many nasty things.

Peters thrashed in his sheets, begged forgiveness, and forgiven this time, once again plunged to the bottom until morning, confused in the reflections of the crooked mirrors of the magic theater.

When a new person appeared in the library, dark and perfumed, in a berry-colored dress, Peters grew agitated. He went to the barber and had his colorless hair cut, then swept his apartment an extra time, and switched the chest of drawers and armchair around. Not that he expected Faina to come over right away; but just in case, Peters had to be ready.

At work there was a New Year's party, and Peters bustled about, cutting out snowflakes the size of saucers and pasting them on the library windows, hanging pink crepe paper, getting tangled in foil icicles, the small Christmas tree lights were reflected in his rolling eyes, it smelled of pine and garlic, and dry snow came through the open window. He thought: if she has, say, a fiancé, I could come over to him, quietly take him by the hand and ask in a regular, man-to-man way: leave Faina, leave her for me, what's it to you, you can find someone else for yourself, you know how to do it. But I don't, my mother ran off with a scoundrel, my father's floating in the sky with blue women, Grandmother ate Grandfather with the rice porridge, ate my childhood, my only childhood, and girls with warts don't want to sit on the couch with me. Come on, give me something, huh?

The burning candles stood, chest-high in translucent apple light, a promise of goodness and peace, the pink-yellow flame nodded its head, champagne fizzed, Faina sang to guitar accompaniment, Dostoevsky's picture on the wall averted its eyes; then they told fortunes, opening Pushkin at random. Peters got: "Adele, love my reed." They laughed at him and asked him to introduce them to Adele; they forgot about it, talking on their own, and he sat quietly in the corner, crunching on cake, figuring out how he would see Faina home. As the party broke up, he ran after her to the coat room, held her fur coat in outstretched arms, watched her change shoes, putting her foot in colored stocking into the cozy fur-lined boot, wrapping a white scarf around her head, and hoisting her bag on her shoulder—everything excited him. She slammed the door, and he saw only her—she waved a mitten, jumped

into the trolley, and vanished in the white blizzard. But even
that was like a promise.

Triumphant bells rang in his ears, and his eye saw what had
previously been invisible. All roads led to Faina, all winds
trumpeted her glory, shouted out her dark name, whirled over
the steep slate roofs, over towers and spires, snaked in snowy
strands and threw themselves at her feet, and the whole city,
all the islands and the water and embankments, statues and
gardens, bridges and fences, wrought-iron roses and horses,
everything blended into a circle, weaving a rattling winter
wreath for his beloved.

He could never manage to be alone with her and he sought
her out on the street, but she always whizzed past him like the
wind, a ball, a snowball thrown by a strong arm. And her
friend who looked in at the library in the evenings was
horrible, impossible, like a toothache—an outgoing journalist,
all creaking leather, long-legged, long-haired, full of international jokes about a Russian, a German, and a Pole
measuring the fatness of their women and the Russian
winning. The journalist wrote an article in the paper, where he
lied and said that "it is always very crowded at the stands with
books on beet raising" and that "visitors call librarian Faina A.
the pilot of the sea of books." Faina laughed, happy to be in
the newspaper, Peters suffered in silence. He kept mustering
his strength to at last take her by the hand, lead her to his
house, and after a session of passion discuss their future life
together.

Toward the end of winter on a damp, tubercular evening
Peters was drying his hands in the men's room under the hot
blast of air and eavesdropping on Faina talking on the
telephone in the corridor. The dryer shuddered and shut up,
and in the ensuing silence the beloved voice laughed: "No, we
have nothing but women on our staff. Who? . . . Him? . . .

That's not a man; he's a wimp. An endocrinological sissy."

Adele, love my reed. Inside, Peters felt as if he had been run over by a trolley. He looked around at the pathetic yellowed tile, the old mirror, swollen from inside with silver sores, the faucet leaking rust—life had selected the right place for the final humiliation. He wound the scarf around his throat carefully, so as not to catch cold in his glands, wended his way home, felt for his slippers, went to the window, out of which he planned to fall, and pulled the blind. The window was thoroughly taped for the winter and he didn't want to waste his work. Then he turned on the oven, placed his head on the rack with cold bread crumbs, and waited. Who would eat rice porridge in his memory? Then Peters remembered that there hadn't been any gas all day, they were doing repairs, grew furious, with trembling finger dialed the dispatcher and screamed horribly and incoherently about the outrageous service, got into his grandfather's chair and sat there till morning.

In the morning, large snowflakes fell slowly. Peters looked at the snow, at the chastened sky, at the new snow banks, and quietly rejoiced that he would have no more youth.

But a new spring came, through the connecting courtyards, the snows died, a cloying smell of decay came from the soil, blue ripples ran over puddles, and Leningrad's cherry trees once again showered white on the matchbox sailboats and newspaper ships—and did it matter at all where you start a new voyage, in a ditch or an ocean, when spring calls and the wind is the same everywhere? And marvelous were the new galoshes Peters bought—their insides laid with the flesh of flowering fuchsia, the taut rubber shining like patent leather, promising to mark his earthly paths with a chain of waffle ovals no matter where he went in search of happiness. And without hurrying, hands behind his back, he strolled along the stone streets, peering deeply into yellow archways, sniffing the air of canals and rivers; and the evening and Saturday women gave him long looks that boded no good, thinking: here's a sickie, we don't need him.

But he didn't need them, either; but Valentina caught his eyes, small and sinfully young—she was buying spring postcards on the sunny embankment, and the fortunate wind, gusting, built, changed, and rebuilt hairdos on her black, short-cropped head. Peters dogged Valentina's steps, afraid to come too close, afraid of failure. Athletic young men ran up to the beauty, grabbed her, laughing, and she went off with them, bouncing, and Peters saw violets—dark, purple— bought and presented, heard them call her by name—it tore away and flew with the wind, the laughing people turned the corner, and Peters was left with nothing—dumpy, white, unloved. And what could he have said to her—to her, so young, so bevioleted? Come up on his flabby legs and offer his flabby hand: "Peter-s . . ." (What a strange name . . ." "My grandmother . . ." "Why did your grandmother . . ." "A little German . . ." "You know German?" "No, but Grand- mother . . .")

Ah, if only he had learned German then! Oh then, probably . . . Then, of course . . . Such a difficult language, it hisses, clicks, and moves around in the mouth, O Tannenbaum, probably no one even knows it. . . . But Peters will go and learn it and astonish the beauty. . . .

Looking over his shoulder for the police, he posted notices on street lamps: "German Lessons Wanted." They hung all through the summer, fading, moving their pseudopods. Peters visited his native lampposts, touching up the letters washed

away by rain, gluing the torn corners, and in late fall he was
called, and it was like a miracle—from the sea of humanity
two floated up, responding to his quiet, faint call, slanted
purple on white. Hey, did you call? I did, I did! He rejected
the persistent and deep-voiced one, who dissolved once more
into oblivion, while he thoroughly questioned the tinny lady,
Elizaveta Frantsevna from Vasiliyevsky Island: how to get
there, where exactly, and how much, and was there a dog, for
he was afraid of dogs.

Everything was settled, Elizaveta Frantsevna expected him
in the evening, and Peters went to his favorite corner to wait
for Valentina—he had been watching and he knew she would
come by as usual, waving her gym bag, at twenty to four, and
would hop into the big red building, and would work out on
the beam amid others like her, swift and young. She would
pass, not suspecting that Peters existed, that he had a great
plan, that life was marvelous. He decided that the best way
would be to buy a bouquet, a big yellow bouquet, and
silently, that was important, silently but with a bow hand it
to Valentina on the familiar corner. "What's this? Ah!"—and
so on.

The wind was blowing, swirling, and it was pouring when
he came out on the embankment. Through the veil of rain the
red barrier of the damp fortress showed murkily, its lead spire
murkily raised its index finger. It had been pouring since last
night, and they had laid in a generous supply of water up
there. The Swedes, when they left these rotten shores, forgot
to take away the sky, and now they probably gloated on their
neat little peninsula—they had clear, blue frost, black firs and
white rabbits, while Peters was coughing here amid the
granite and mildew.

In the fall, Peters took great pleasure in hating his home
town, and the city repaid him in kind: it spat icy streams from

pounding roof tops, filling his eyes with opaque, dark flows, shoved especially damp and deep puddles under his feet, slapped the cheeks of his nearsighted face, his felt hat, and his tummy with lashes of rain. The slimy buildings that bumped into Peters were purposely covered with tiny white mushrooms and a mossy toxic velvet, and the wind, which had come from big highwayman roads, tumbled around his soggy feet in deathly tubercular figure eights.

He took his post with the bouquet, and October poured from the skies, and his galoshes were like bathtubs, and the newspaper wrapped three times around the expensive yellow flowers fell apart into shreds, the time came and went and Valentina did not come and would not come but he stood there chilled through to his underwear, to his white hairless body sprinkled with tender red birthmarks.

The clock struck four. Peters shoved his bouquet in a garbage can. Why wait? He understood it was stupid and too late to learn German, that the lovely Valentina, brought up among athletic and vernal youths, would merely laugh and step over him, lumpy and broadwaisted; not for him were fiery passions and light steps, fast dances and leaps on the beam, or casually bought damp April violets, or the sunny wind from the gray waters of the Neva, or laughter and youth; that all attempts were futile, that he should have married his own grandmother and quietly melted away in the warm room to the ticking of the clock, eating sugar buns and planting his old stuffed rabbit in front of his plate for coziness and amusement.

He was hungry, and he went to the first friendly light he saw, bought some soup, and sat down next to two beauties eating patties with onions and blowing away the foggy skin on their cooling pinkish cocoa.

The girls were chattering about love, of course, and Peters heard the story of a certain Irochka, who had been working a

long time on a comrade from fraternal Yemen, or maybe
Kuwait, in hopes that he would marry her. Irochka had heard
that there in the sandy steppes of the Arabian land, oil was as
plentiful as berries, every decent man was a millionaire and
flew in his own jet with a gold toilet seat. It was that gold seat
that drove Irochka crazy, for she grew up in the Yaroslavl
region, where the conveniences were three walls without the
fourth with a view of the pea field; all in all, it was like Ilya
Repin's painting *Space*. But the Arab was in no hurry to wed,
and when Irochka put it to him straight, he replied in the vein
of, "Oh, yeah, your mother wears army boots. So long,
sucker!" and so on, and tossed Irochka out with her pathetic
belongings. The girls paid no attention to Peters, and he
listened and felt sorry for the unknown Irochka and pictured
the pea-covered expanses of Yaroslavl, trimmed around the
horizon with dark, wolf-filled forests, melting in the blissful
silence under the blue shimmer of the northern sun, or the
dry, grim squeak of millions of sand grains, the taut push of
a desert hurricane, the brown light through the deep murk,
forgotten white palaces filmed with mortal dust or enchanted
by long-dead sorcerers.

The girls moved to the story of the complicated relationship
of Olya and Valery, of Anyuta's heartlessness, and Peters,
drinking his broth, listened openly, entering someone else's
story invisibly, he came in close contact with someone's
secrets, he was standing at the door with bated breath, he felt,
smelled, and saw, as if in a magical movie, and it was all
unbearably accessible—just reach out—flickering faces, tears
in injured eyes, explosions of smiles, sunlight in hair, cascad-
ing pink and green sparks, dust motes in the ray and the heat
of warmed parquet floors, creaking nearby, in that strange,
happy, and lively life.

"We're done, let's go!" one beauty commanded the other,

and spreading their transparent umbrellas, like signs of another, higher existence, they floated out into the rain and rose into the skies, into the blue beyond the clouds, hidden from his eyes.

Peters selected a rough piece of cardboard from the plastic glass serving as napkin holder and wiped his mouth. Life roared by, bypassing him, and hurried on, like a swift-flowing river goes around a heavy mound of rocks.

The cleaning woman whirled like a sand storm among the tables, flipped her rag in Peters's face, and deftly picked up twenty dirty dishes and disappeared in the yeasty air.

"It's not my fault," Peters said to someone. "It's not my fault at all. I want to participate. But they won't take me. No one wants to play with me. Why? But I'll try harder, I'll win!"

He went out—under icy splashes, under the cold, lashing water. I'll win. Win. I'll clench my teeth and push on through. And I will learn that damned language. There, on Vasiliyevsky Island, in the dampest of Leningrad's damp, Elizaveta Frantsevna is waiting, swimming like a seal or mermaid, mumbling easily in the dark German tongue. He would come and they would chatter together. O Tannenbaum! O, I repeat, Tannenbaum! How does it go after that? I'll find out when I get there.

Oh, well, farewell Valentina and her quick sister, ahead lies only an old German woman—he braced himself. . . . Peters imagined his path, his looplike track in the wet city, and failure, running on his tail, sniffing the waffle prints of his shoes, and the old woman at the end of his path, and in order to confuse fate he hailed a taxi and sailed through the rain—steam rose from his feet, the driver was grim, and he wanted to get out right away. *Tacka-tacka-tacka-tacka,* ticked away his money.

"Stop here."

A doorman guarded the entrance to a gilded place—a door into a subcellar, and beyond it muffled music blared, and lamps shone in the windows like long tubes of acid syrup. Young men—all pretenders for Valentina's hand, farewell Valentina—huddled in front of the door, teeth chattering in the whirlwinds of rain, there was no room in the restaurant, but the doorman, deceived by Peters's solid appearance, let him in, and Peters passed through and two others slipped in by his side. A good place. Peters took off his hat and raincoat in a dignified manner, promised a tip with his eyes, stepped into the noisy room, and trumpeted his arrival in his hand-kerchief. A fine place. He ordered a pink cocktail, a pagoda pastry, drank, ate, drank some more and relaxed. A very, very fine place. And at his elbow appeared a moth-girl, from out of thin air, from the colored cigarette smoke; her red, green dress—the colored lights blinked—blossomed on her like an orchid, and her eyelashes blinked like wings, and bracelets jangled on her thin arms, and she was completely loyal to Peters to her dying breath. He signaled for more pink alcohol, afraid to speak, to scare off the girl, the marvelous Peri, the flying flower, and they sat in silence, as amazed by each other as would be a goat and an angel upon meeting.

He waved his hand—and they gave even more and some meat.

"Ahem," said Peters, praying to heaven not to recall its messenger right away. "As a child I had a stuffed bunny—a friend in fact and I promised him so much. And now I'm off to my German lesson, ahem."

"I like stuffed bunnies, they're really cute," the Peri noted coldly.

Peters was surprised by the angel's stupidity—a stuffed bunny couldn't be cute, he was either a friend or a nonentity, a sack of sawdust.

"And we also played cards and I always got the cat," Peters recalled.

"Cats are really cute, too," the girl replied through her teeth, like a familiar lesson, looking over the crowd.

"No! Why do you say that?" Peters countered, getting upset. "That's not the point. I'm not talking about that, I'm talking about life, it keeps teasing you, showing and taking away, showing and taking away. You know, it's like a shop window, it shines and it's locked, and you can't take anything. And, I ask, why not?"

"You're really cute, too," the indifferent girl insisted, not listening. "You dropped something."

When he finally got up from the table, the angel had risen to heaven, and with it, Peters's wallet and money. Got it. Well. So be it. Peters sat with his leftovers, as immobile as a suitcase, sobering up, imagining how he would have to explain, ask—the scorn and mockery of the coat check—fish for damp rubles in the swampy pockets of his raincoat, shaking out change that slipped fishlike into the lining. . . . The music machine stomped and beat the drums, announcing someone's coming passion. The cocktail evaporated through his ears. *Cuc-koo!* There.

What are you, life? A silent theater of Chinese shadows, a chain of dreams, a charlatan's store? Or a gift of unrequited love—that's all that is intended for me? What about happiness? What is happiness? Ingrate, you're alive, you weep love strive fall and that's not enough? What? . . . Not enough? Oh, is that so? There isn't anything else.

"I'm waiting! I'm waiting!" shouted Elizaveta Frantsevna, a quick, curly-haired lady, throwing back latches and bolts, letting in the robbed Peters, dark, dangerous, full of misery up to his throat, to his top tight button.

"This way. Let's start right away. Sit down on the couch. First lotto, then tea. All right? Quickly take a card. Who has a goat? I have a goat? Who has a guinea hen?"

I'm going to kill her, decided Peters. Elizaveta Frantsevna, look away, I'm going to kill you. You, and my late grandmother, and the girl with warts, and Valentina, and the fake angel, and all those others—all of them who promised and tricked me, seduced and abandoned me; I'll kill them in the name of all fat and wheezy, tongue-tied and awkward men, in the name of all of those locked in the dark closet, all those not invited to the party, get ready, Elizaveta Frantsevna, I'm going to smother you with that embroidered pillow. And no one will ever know.

"Frantsevna!" someone shouted and pounded on the door. "Give me three rubles, I'll wash the hallway for you."

The urge passed, Peters put aside the pillow. He wanted to sleep. The old woman rustled her money, Peters looked down at the "Domestic Animals" card.

"What are you thinking about? Who has a cat?"

"I have a cat," Peters said. "Who else has one?" And he sidled out, crushing the cardboard cat in his fist. The hell with life. Sleep, sleep, fall asleep and don't wake up.

Spring came and spring went and came again, and spread out blue flowers in the meadows and waved her hand and called through his sleep, "Peters! Peters!" but he slept soundly and heard nothing.

Summer rustled, wandered free in gardens, sitting on benches, swinging bare feet in the dust, calling Peters out on the warm street, the hot sidewalks; whispered, sparkling in the shimmer of linden trees, in the flutter of poplars; called, didn't get an answer, and left, dragging its hem, into the light part of the horizon.

Life got on tiptoe and peered into the window in surprise: why was Peters asleep, why wasn't he coming out to play its cruel games?

But Peters slept and slept and lived in his dream: neatly wiping his mouth, he ate vegetables and drank dairy products; he shaved his dull face—around his shut mouth and under his sleeping eyes—and once, accidentally, in passing, he married a cold, hard woman with big feet, with a dull name. The woman regarded people severely, knowing that people were crooks, that you couldn't trust anyone; her basket held dry bread.

She took Peters with her everywhere, holding his hand tight, the way his grandmother once did, on Sundays they went to the zoological museum, into the resonant, polite halls—to look at still, woolen mice or the white bones of a whale; on weekdays they went out to stores, bought dead yellow macaroni, old people's brown soap, and watched heavy vegetable oil pour through the narrow funnel, as thick as depression, endless and viscous, like the sands of the Arabian desert.

"Tell me," the woman asked severely, "are the chickens chilled? Give me that one." And "that one" is placed in the old shopping bag, and sleeping Peters carried home the cold young chicken, who had known neither love nor freedom, nor green grass nor the merry round eye of a girlfriend. And at home, under the watchful eye of the hard woman, Peters himself had to open up the chest of the chilled creature with knife and axe and tear out the slippery purplish heart, the red roses of the lungs, and the blue breathing stalk, in order to wipe out the memory in the ages of the one who was born and hoped, moved his young wings and dreamed of a green royal tail, of pearl grains, of the golden dawn over the waking world.

The summers and winters slipped by and melted, dissolving

and fading, harvests of rainbows hung over distant houses, young greedy blizzards marauded from the northern forests, moving time forward, and the day came when the woman with big feet abandoned Peters, quietly shutting the door and leaving to buy soap and stir pots for another. Then Peters carefully opened his eyes and woke up.

The clock was ticking, fruit compote floated in a glass pitcher, and his slippers had grown cold overnight. Peters felt himself, counted his fingers and hairs. Regret flickered and passed. His body still remembered the quiet of past years, the heavy sleep of the calendar, but in the depths of his spiritual flesh something long forgotten, young and trusting, was stirring, sitting up, shaking itself and smiling.

Old Peters pushed the window frame—the blue glass rang, a thousand yellow birds flew up, and the naked golden spring cried, laughing: catch me, catch me! New children played in the puddles with their buckets. And wanting nothing, regretting nothing, Peters smiled gratefully at life—running past, indifferent, ungrateful, treacherous, mocking, meaningless, alien—marvelous, marvelous, marvelous.

A NOTE ON THE TYPE

The text of this book was set in a digitized
version of Garamond No. 3, first cut by Claude
Garamond (c. 1480–1561). Garamond was a
pupil of Geoffroy Tory and is believed to have
based his letters on the Venetian models, although he introduced a number of important
differences, and it is to him we owe the letter
we know as "old style." He gave to his letters a
certain elegance and a feeling of movement that
won for their creator an immediate reputation
and the patronage of Francis I of France.

Composed by American–Stratford Graphic
Services, Inc., Brattleboro, Vermont. Printed
and bound by Fairfield Graphics, Fairfield,
Pennsylvania.

Designed by Anthea Lingeman